Opium Poppy

Some Books from Social Science Press and Aurum Books

Opium Poppy

by
Hubert Haddad
A Novel

Translated from the French by Renuka George

AN IMPRINT
OF SOCIAL
SCIENCE PRESS

SOCIAL
SCIENCE
PRESS

Published by

Esha Béteille
SOCIAL SCIENCE PRESS
69 Jor Bagh, New Delhi 110 003

Copyright © Éditions Zulma
Copyright to the English translation © (2014) Renuka George and
Social Science Press

Originally published as OPIUM POPPY

ÉDITIONS ZULMA
18, rue du Dragon –75006
Paris
France

ISBN: 978-93-83166-06-0

The Work is published via the Publication Assistance Programme Tagore, with the support of the Institut Français en Inde/ Ambassade de France en Inde and the Institut Français de Paris.

Social Science Press gratefully acknowledges the generous financial support from Nine Dot Nine Mediaworx Pvt Ltd towards the publication of this book.

Set in Adobe Garamond 11/14
Typeset by Eleven Arts, Delhi 110 035
Printed by G.H. Prints Pvt Ltd
A-256, Okhla Industrial Area
Phase-1, New Delhi 110 006

Author's Preface

A novel takes shape surreptitiously, over a lifetime sometimes. This process of incubation is called experience. I have long been haunted by the tragedy of child soldiers, probably because I am an immigrant myself. My parents were fairground people and for a while, during my childhood, I had to work hard to earn money in Paris, a frightening place during the Algerian War. Later, I divided my work as a writer between poetic imagination, with fables or fantasy writing, and the current issues of the contemporary world, with novels like *Palestine or Opium Poppy*. I am in no sense a journalist, although my heroes are often investigative reporters working in the field. Personally, when it comes to a novel, I am unable to work with what I have seen, as I need to invent the places, to dream of them until they take shape. Strangely, my travels are only indirectly useful in this process. I have been to Kerala several times, to Cochin, in search of the Jewish Kingdom of Cranganore. Will I write this novel that means a lot to me, someday?

I travelled the length and breadth of Rwanda, up to the Congolese border, meeting people who had witnessed the genocide, school children and visiting memorials. I had thought of focusing my novel on child soldiers, but on my return, I was so devastated by what I had seen and heard, the only thing I could write was a feature story. Tragedy is universal; today there are three hundred thousand child soldiers all over the world. So it was in Asia, Afghanistan, that my story suddenly took shape, enriched by my visit to Rwanda. For a long while in Paris, one would meet little Afghani refugees under the bridges or the elevated metro. They were totally destitute. I have not forgotten their faces.

The child in *Opium Poppy,* could be one of them, a ten year old, whose journey I retraced from the Pashtun region of Kandahar. From poppy cultivation by poor farmers, to international drug dealers, indoctrination by the Taliban and begging in the suburbs of large towns, we discover what half a century of total warfare implies for the children, who are always its first victims. Wars that involve money, weapons, fanaticism and invasive alliance politics. Before deciding on the title *Opium Poppy*, the poppy flower, that evokes the fragility of living things and the manner in which they can be used for destruction, I thought of calling this novel *The child you will become*, to emphasise the collective responsibility that we, as adults, have in shaping the destiny of the world.

Hubert Haddad
(Translated by Renuka George)

They gave me a revolver and when I pulled the trigger
I saw I had shot my brother

BERTOLT BRECHT

1

Again and again they ask him his name. The first time, some people sitting down had recited all the names beginning with the letter A. For no reason, they had stopped at Alam. Maybe because he looked so scared. If they had begun at the end and had stopped at Zia, his eyes would have grown just as wide. To make them happy though, he had repeated after them the two syllables of the word Alam. That was right in the beginning. He had just been caught on a station platform as he got off a train.

The lady before him has straw hair and a porcelain smile. She holds her pen by both its ends, just above a blue grey file, full of boxes to be filled in. "And your first name is Alam, is that right?" His first name, the cats call him *meow* when he sleeps on a roof, it's *woof* for the dogs he tames with stolen sugar in garages, it could even be the tawny owl's call in forest nights. Why doesn't she tell him what her name is? Everyone wants him to nod his head, backwards and forwards like an overburdened mule. Alam, that was his brother, there, in the mountains. The blond lady has got up, she points to an iron bench. "Now get undressed". He does not understand and shies away from the bench. "Come on, take all that off!" she says, pulling on his collar. He turns his back on her with a determined pout, hugging his elbows close to his body to prevent her from stealing his anorak. What was the point of giving it to him? If they want to take it back, they should return his old jacket. He would transfer his fortune to it. Everything he owns fits into his pockets. The lady laughs apologetically behind him. "Come on, hurry up then, I am going to examine you!" Still ill at ease, he lets his arms fall to his sides. "You, daktar?" he asks with a sudden change of heart. To confirm it, she takes a stethoscope out of a sliding drawer and hangs it around her neck. Her earrings tinkle against the aluminium. The child has turned pale. He complies without too much hesitation, as if the examination instrument were a weapon. Naked, his knees trembling slightly, he allows her to touch him, as skittish as a sheep in a shearing shed. "I'm not going to eat you", murmurs the lady doctor, pressing a curved scar shaped like a magnifying glass lens, just under his left breast, with her index finger. She lets her finger slip towards another bullet hole in the hollow of his shoulder blade, and finally, she feels his neck, near the half torn off earlobe. "It looks as if they almost got you there!" These words, she repeats them several times, studying the enigma of this highly sensitive constellation: three scars of the same size, aligned like Orion's belt. To reassure the child as she handles him, the doctor begins to chat calmly, not expecting any particular response; it is like an improvised chant. The child listens with the gravity of a caged animal. "There are so many refugees like yourself who have fled the war, entire families, orphans, widows, criminals too. But you must help us. You must tell us your story. How could we ever find your relatives if you don't help us? We know so little: you come from a village in the South, in the Kandahar region; you showed it to us on the map. What happened? Why did you leave? I wonder how you managed to survive this machine gun attack, it looks like an execution; usually they only massacre men. The kids are either recruited or abandoned. You have nothing to be afraid of any more. Our role is to protect you; you're safe from the bad people. You'll learn the language we speak here. We'll educate you. We'll give you a profession, a future…"

The child looks at the excessively white hands on his skin. Buffalo bones in the desert used to be this colour. He is amazed that they are interested in his old wounds. They no longer bleed; they no longer hurt him. That happened months ago. Soon, he will shoot up suddenly, like his brother, like One Eyed Alam, before he was recruited.

In the literacy class a little later, he obediently answers to this name by which they keep calling him. Something inside him is even satisfied: Alam is no longer completely dead. His name, repeated by the stranger on the dais, echoes deep within him and when he nods his head it is with his wounded face. Today the teacher writes the date, the third of November, on the blackboard. He explains the meaning of the words *to be*. It is a verb: conjugating it imbues it with certain powers. Every action takes place thanks to this verb: without it, nothing really exists. There would be no relationships. *I am, you are, he is, we are…* Why do we always have to falter through interminable recitations of other people's languages and deny, choke back our own words, our own songs? Since he was captured he has been treated like the offspring of imaginary parents. They teach him things that are unreal. Children only serve to please adults. All around him the pupils smile at the teacher, they want to be hugged, especially the girls. Except for the one in the first row, the tall one with braids thicker than a horse's mane. Hunched forward, her expression is that of a sad, broken puppet, with sharp bones sticking out of her bird-like shoulders. Sometimes when she emerges from a dream to answer a question, her clear voice surprises everyone. She speaks with a gaiety that her body cannot endure. The little white kids, the ones from Serbia or Kosovo, tease her about her black, smooth skin, but she ignores them, it even amuses her. There are splinters of ivory in her wise panther's gaze. They say her whole family burned while she watched, during a sudden revival of the civil war on her country's borders. That is the story she tells.

She is Diwani the Tutsi. A group of stragglers belonging to the defeated Interahamwe militia caught up with her; they caught up with her and she was raped by the hordes with their long knives, recruited amongst football supporters.

"Who can make a sentence for me in the simple past, with the verb *to be*?" The teacher guilelessly questions the classroom full of lost children. One would think he was asking for forgiveness, hoping for someone to say to him: "it's not your fault; keep persecuting us with your simple past". Tall, with large hands, he gesticulates on the dais with his head and his arms. The past is never so simple. The events have taken place thousands of times. It is not so easy to find one's way through the maze of torturers, recruiters, border escorts, customs officers, informers, and police. And who can swear they actually carried out such an act at a specific moment? Diwani recites the verb to save, as she is asked to: *I saved, you saved, he saved...* She stops in a whimper and hides her face in her hands. Even the little white kids no longer laugh. Embarrassed, the teacher declares the lesson over.

At the Camir, the acronym in blue letters which stands for *Centre d'accueil des mineurs isolés et réfugiés,* (Reception Centre for Isolated and Juvenile Refugees), a detention centre like any other, the little white kids from the East European countries reign over the dormitories and the canteen. The others, from Africa or Asia, do not have enough in common. To create a gang, you need at least three people and you have to speak the same language. There are about half a dozen little white kids, they have suffered every experience related to the catastrophy of life and are taking their revenge. More than one has encountered drugs, prostitution and the taste of death. Wolves with steel jaws broke their necks.

Yuko, the leader, barely fifteen years old, gets his pointed ears and his cruciform pupils from them. He claims to have killed a young insolent gypsy with his own hands, one night in a train shed in Belgrade. The others respect him like rejected puppies. Yuko cannot bear anyone looking him in the eyes. It makes him uncomfortable, as if someone were touching his stomach. It makes him want to beat someone till he draws blood. He wanders through the Centre's corridors with an unrelenting feeling of abandon. As men have left him nothing to hope for, he will endeavour to become worse than them. He is already working on it with anyone who approaches him, his terrified younger brothers and all the refugees from nowhere. To fetter someone is to hold them to ransom at every moment. Yuko knows full well that if the administration managed to identify him, he would be removed from this place and sent to a detention centre for minor convicts. He is accused of enough offences and repeat offences in distant places, in other countries, as well as trifles where he is now, some of them liable to be judged by a correctional court. Sometimes not having any legal document is an advantage. None of the anthropometric databases can identify him. He knows his rights. According to the Geneva Convention he cannot be expelled. A gnat sometimes manages to escape the spider web of the law.

Yuko hates the boarding school atmosphere at the Camir—a combination of young people's home and transit camp. But there are no dons with switchblades or shotguns, nor an older sister hooked on drugs demanding money: at least they leave him in peace. He will escape before they think of trying him. A tree with no leaves sways in the wind, in a solitary recess in the garden. His forehead pressed against a window, the adolescent watches the game two magpies play, hopping from branch to branch despite the storm. Ashen clouds nudge the roofs of working class houses, set in a row under the angular horizon of an industrial zone.

Just then, the patter of light footsteps brings his gaze back to the window dripping with condensation, then to the bend in the corridor. Slender Diwani advances without seeing him. She does not notice men or their sons and meanders through a world split in two. "Stop!" shouts Yuko, grabbing her wrist. He laughs with a cold rage that has nothing to do with the moment, and twists the girl's arm forcing her to her knees. Despite the pain she does not submit. The night of her pupils covers the chalky face. "What do you want from me?" she says dully. He releases her and would like to continue to laugh but wants to prolong the moment, forcing himself not to strike her. "Nothing, I don't want anything, I hate you, I hate all of you, the darkies, the wogs, the Chinks! Get out or I'll murk you!" Diwani studies the painful rictus at the bottom of this face and remembers the last man, the one who was supposed to kill her when they'd all finished gasping over her. It was in a terribly bleak camp, on the other side of the border, far from her hills.

Attracted by a silhouette behind the window, they turn away. A spark of complicity runs through this silent staring match. Someone is walking on the lawn down below. It is the nameless kid, the one they call Alam. He seems to be counting his footsteps, as if to locate a hidden treasure. Everyone in the Centre is worried about him, his staring eyes, the silence that surrounds him. At the age of eleven or twelve there is nothing he enjoys, his lips churn stony syllables, both his hands seem to be tightly clasped around a very heavy stone that is crushing his ribs. All his attention is focused on the sky or the earth, studiously avoiding people. Nothing escapes him though. He seems to soak up presences, like a sponge. And then he disappears in a ghostly breath.

In fact he is gone. Diwani and Yuko's glances brush against each other again, disbelieving, then return to the yellowing lawn. This window onto the garden seals a sort of pact between them, connected to the premonition of the moment. "Get off now!" says Yuko, embarrassed at having been seen through, even if only for the blink of an eye.

2

Trapped by immobility, Alam, the wrongly named, loses himself in the same pain every night. He had been christened the 'Unconscious' there. Curled up on his iron bed, he spends hours trying to escape the inferno of the dreams. The sky the colour of fire is the first image. The sky burns the cracked earth, a vast deserted conch encircled by blue mountains.

It was in the Sangin area, a few dozen miles from a military advanced base. The rebels had waited till dawn to attack the village. Rocks towered over the hills, like the ruins of a fortress. The first explosions caused little concern, as the roar of bombers flying at low altitude rocked the region so terribly day and night. The crackle of automatic weapons though, finally roused the sleeping population. Panic stricken families were jumping out of windows and already running towards the poppy fields. Within seconds, the assailant focused his firepower. The farmers were falling like rag dolls under the bullets. Sulphur dust seemed to rise from these bundles rolling on the ground. A woman hit in the neck began to scream madly beneath her veil; blood was running over the fabric, onto her breast, a mother's breast. Hands over their ears, two small, terrified children in a corner were pleading with her. Other women were fleeing towards the road, following a herd of sheep. A hobbled donkey brayed adamantly amidst the descending wave of insurgents clutching Kalashnikovs in their fists. Grenades silenced the cries in a shed. As soon as a farmer emerged from a doorway, a well-aimed shot cut him down. The children were banging into the attackers' legs; they were climbing over the bodies to run towards the hills.

The noise of automatic weapons ceased just as suddenly in a commotion. A turbaned war chief had given the order to fall back. The throb of the blades of the fighter helicopters was audible: the coalition forces had been informed somehow and were sending in their explosive parade. With reptilian speed, the armed group scattered in the escarpment. For a few minutes longer, the bombs and machine gun fire futilely swept the deserted foothills.

Other helicopters, without missile launchers this time, landed in a wormwood field near the buildings. Preceded by armed men, uniformed stretcher-bearers and doctors ran through an undulating mirage. The dawn sun unfurled the wan mountains in the distance, like tarpaulin over tents in a transit camp. The din of weapons and rotor blades gave way to a deathly silence. There was the sound of suppressed coughs and contained tears Everyone feared an ambush by a concealed suicide bomber, seeking to cover his comrades' retreat. The wounded were transported to the shelter of the aircraft cabins even before they had been identified. They were evacuated rapidly while a parachute commando, dropped by a troop plane, locked down the sector. Sporadic shots still echoed around the hills. The donkey had not stopped braying. There were other cries, higher pitched; in a movement of reverse panic the women who had dispersed to the shelter of caves or fallen rocks, were now running towards the village with its three alleys filled with the corpses of men and sheep.

An army doctor and a nurse had stayed behind with the commando; they walked around the low stone walls sheltering shacks made of rammed earth. Most of the wounded had taken refuge in their homes after the raid, those who were not too badly hurt. Several refused the Canadians' help. The doctor handed out compresses and antiseptic. An old man, as thin as a stork, a white beard twisted between his fingers, allowed them to look at his foot. A shard of a rocket had broken some of his bones. While they were attaching the splints, he smiled through all his wrinkles as if they were paying him a courtesy call. A vestige of irony sparkled in the man's eyes. The doctor's hair had just slipped out of her cap. Mechanically, the major pushed the strands back behind her ear. At that moment someone called to her urgently from a window, its glass panes replaced by squares of oil paper. "Helen, over here, quick! There's a kid, he's badly hurt!"

The sun overlooked the mountains that stood out in high, petrified waves above the low ochre walls. In a recess in the labyrinth, at the back of a courtyard, the huddled child seemed to be dead. "He's breathing" claimed the nurse. The woman in uniform knelt down and tore his tunic open with both her hands. She recoiled slightly. "Three bullets, a direct hit. It looks like an execution. I thought they only went after men…" A helicopter was called for urgently from the base. As she attached the needle to a syringe, she studied the small quivering body with a sense of hopelessness. Death wanted to take him and they could do nothing but count the minutes. In the field for a year, Major Helen had not yet got used to closing children's eyes. She had had to learn to repress her emotions. Wounded flesh did not have a soul; it was a thing, beaten down by the sticky sap of pain. At least she wanted to believe so, after being present at the deaths of so many, both assassins and victims. Helen found it difficult to bear the enigmatic dignity of the youngest in that moment, as if they had always known the absurdity of living. Dressed in the usual old clothes illiterate mountain shepherds wear, this one, oddly, had solid leather sandals on his feet. His eyes closed, he was bleeding from the nose and the lips; an expression of infinite detachment hovered over this handsome face, about to be transformed into a mask of dust.

Back from their mission, the heavy fighter helicopters chopped up the azure above the illuminated slopes. For a moment the major had hoped the emergency helicopter had arrived. The Tigers tacked around the escarpment at low altitude before shooting off towards the military base near Salavat. Large birds soon took their place, scavengers soaring with incomparable grace in the kerosene-saturated air.

Concealed by their veils, the village women were now running from one house to the next, screaming, beseeching God. The oldest were on their knees before the shacks, slapping their faces, ululating. Weapons hanging across their chests, the soldiers were laying out the corpses on the forecourt of a mosque. Others, on the look out, patrolled the low walls and the fields. The male nurse who had returned to the child's side, had called out to two or three women gathered around a well. They had all evaded the question, seeming not to understand. "His family will know where to find him, dead or alive!" he says, pointing to a large insect throbbing at the edge of the horizon. When the emergency helicopter landed, Major Helen felt the child's pulse again. His heartbeat was barely stronger than an eyelid reacting to a light touch. "It would be a miracle" is all she says.

3

A woman with elongated eyes, like a cat or a fox, has been questioning him for an unknown length of time. She calls him Alam, in a slightly hoarse voice. Every question she asks him ends with Alam. It does not bother him, but he trembles secretly. His hands are damp. The woman shows him pictures. "What do you see in these shapes?" She offers him colour pencils and sheets of white paper. "You're going to make three drawings for me. First, what it was like before the war, then what it was like during the war, and finally, what it will be like after the war." He doesn't mind drawing. You can hide your face in the symbols. He likes the colour yellow, but it is never yellow enough. He presses down on the point so hard that it breaks. Three times in a row, the woman sitting opposite him sharpens the pencil again with the blade of a tiny knife. That was before, but the war never had a beginning; it comes and goes like a storm. Yellow reminds him of home when the open windows let in the sunshine and the swallows. Blue could cover the sheet of paper, but the night is within him. And then black invades everything with its centipedes' feet. He never uses red, red tears him up inside. When the woman holds the colour pencil out to him, he notices her nails that are of the same colour. Her nails and her lips that move above the knife. He does not want to make a third drawing. He shakes his head. He's too tired now. "You'll do it next time" says the child psychiatrist from the health service attached to the reception centre. She tidies away the paper and pencils without taking her eyes off the child. The scar under the ear with its torn off lobe certainly explains his sullen attitude. Everything he has been through is better revealed by his demeanour than by any India ink or colour pencil test. Nonetheless, there is still a certain naivety in young Alam's attitude, the kind one sees in young bears or wolves. The difference is he no longer knows how to play. He took no pleasure in drawing and look at how he rocks himself on his chair! The young woman represses a desire to shrug her shoulders: fortunately her capacity for critical thought is as strong as her sentimentalism.

A short while later, she will record the risks of 'differed psycho-traumatic stress disorder' in young Alam X's computerised file. She will highlight her conclusions in red: *fear of annihilation, withdrawal from touch, characteristic insensitivity to emotional stimuli, emotional anaesthesia, general difficulty in adapting...*

Back in the literacy class, Alam experiences the same sensation as the other time, before the lady doctor with her straw-coloured hair. The oil on these naked faces, these manicured hands, like those of festival dolls, these fragrances of unknown flowers: everything that emanates from the women in this country seems vaguely bewitched to him. They frighten and attract him as if they were gutless giants. Something in them is missing, a flame, a commotion, but their icy presence scares him a bit. The first time, when he had found himself wandering along the sheltered boulevards of Kabul's wealthy areas, the tall, pale mannequins in the windows had intimidated him in the same way. Like dead women from another world. In his memory, a strange wound surrendered to the breath of night, only veils remain.

He remembers the little rag girls and all those women, widows of the sun, who quickly stripped off their mourning clothes as soon as they shut the door. Indoors or outdoors, all the women fussed about with lengths of cloth, they were constantly washing them and wearing them, they spread them in the wind and folded them up again. For their new-born and their dead, for the children's bed and for party dresses, they were constantly cutting up fabric, which they stitched and embroidered. It was like a caterpillars' or wasps' nest in the house, all this cloth piling up. A peaceful spiders' workshop.

The women here are more like huge dragonflies. They fly on the spot with their hair and their hands outspread, never taking their glass eyes off you.

The teacher turned confidently towards him. He wants a sentence with the verb 'to be', conjugated in the present. "*Tou yak bandé asté! Tou yak bandé asté!*" shouts Alam the Unconscious, amidst laughter. The teacher does not understand his language. He does not understand Soninke and Bambara either. "I can't either, I can't speak properly, I am alone", says beautiful Diwani who has come to his rescue. The teacher's expression loses some of its severity and he smiles. "Tomorrow we will learn the future" he concludes, wiping the blackboard. All the pupils, big and small, from Mali and Togo, from Pakistan, the Kurds from Anatolia, the pale refugees from Caucasia, stand up in a single movement, as if released from a crushing weight of indignity. In the corridors they return to the irresolute attitudes born of confusion. Some push each other violently, gasping, spitting insults. Alam distances himself from them. He does not want to respond to Yuko's shoves. His hands stuck in the pockets of his anorak, in one he clutches the empty case of a spent bullet from a Soviet assault rifle, in the other, his stone heart, a rough emerald crystal brought back from the mountains. He has no idea what either of these objects is doing in his pockets, but he hangs on to them as if they were the keys to a world.

Diwani sits down opposite him in the refectory. She fills his glass with water. "It looks as if you don't understand anything on purpose", she jokes. "Eat your mash then..." She laughs as he frowns. This slip of a man, she enjoys teasing him, like the little brothers at the refugee camp. It will be a while before he turns into a wild animal. All men turn into tigers or wolves one day or another. Those who retract their claws are almost worse with their money and their floppy mouths. Diwani remembers the confusing routes of the exodus. With rape and massacre all around, men's desire is like a gift sometimes, a sordid indulgence. Opposite her, Alam contemplates the bewildering landscape of his plate. His eyes wander over it like two awkward beetles. He shivers for no reason, a taste of rust in his throat. Images superimpose themselves over everything, as the associations surface. The nice smooth mash is a young girl's cheek. His gaze loses itself in Diwani's hair that sparkles more brightly than the gutted belly of an anthill.

Then, everything took place in a small mining town in the Kandahar region. Life in these buildings, that resembled terraced farms, where no animals or stables were to be seen, was a change from the silence of the countryside. What was her name, his neighbour with her morning voice? The whole building was proud and jealous of her beauty, although nobody had ever caught so much as a glimpse of her under the veil. The young girl's mother swore to everyone that a flower like this only existed in paradise. Every day since the public school had opened its doors to girls again, she would set off joyfully, as usual, with the other girls, well concealed under the blue fabric of the chadri. They were going to learn one of the male professions that people practiced outside the home. In most families this was prohibited; it was even an offence. They would face insults. The young men in the area would beat them with their fists and their feet. But they wanted to learn to read and to calculate. Every day they set off again gaily to high school. One morning, some boys on a motorcycle blocked their way. They raised the girls' veils. As if in play, they sprayed their faces with water pistols.

Alam scratches the mash with his fork. Fearfully, he suspects a vague connection between his plate and the meanderings of his mind. The beautiful young girls, he imagines them bare-headed, their hair burnt, faces bloody and disfigured like a monkey's bottom. In a single act, vitriol erases the miraculous dew of a face. There is no one left in the house of memory… "What are you thinking about?" asks Diwani. Digging grooves with the teeth of a fork in the plate of mash, is that thinking? " I'm going to leave" he says without thinking. "You want to leave the Centre? We're not allowed to." Outside, she thinks, it's not our country, we, the refugees from hell are not allowed. Here, at least, nobody forces her to sleep with strangers. They do not tear off her clothes to defile her or to take her money. When she was little, there were white or black soldiers everywhere. The nights were uncertain. The elders used to talk about the time of the machetes, exhibiting their weapons, showing how their mother and sisters and the hundreds of thousands, who trembled in terror under the indifferent gaze of the white or black soldiers, had been chopped into little pieces. "You aren't scared to leave with nothing, not even an address?" Alam does not know what to answer. He has been elsewhere for so long. A meat fly explores the edges of his plate. Framed by a window, the branch of a chestnut tree sways in the wind. Birds carved out of the pewter of the sky fly obliquely across copses and roofs. Far away, even further away, is escape. At the end of the land, there are trains and boats. And other lands beyond the seas. "Your ear..." murmurs Diwani. He studies the ivory of her eyes and the brilliant whiteness of her incisors under the thick lip. Can we see with our teeth too? Diwani's skin is as blue as night. Tiny scars form a tree on her left cheek. There are sparks even in her hair. Her lips are moving again: "You should wait until you know how to read. You aren't going to ask the cops which way to go..."

Night is like Diwani as long as his eyes remain open. Lying on his side, in the younger children's dormitory, he watches a moving dot of light through an inaccessible window. It has wire netting across it anyway. The aeroplane gains altitude: headed for America or Australia. He widens his eyes to avoid falling asleep. Sleep is a trap in the insurgent night. He digs his nails into the hollow of his palms. A monitor's gangling silhouette wanders between the beds. It bends over the little white kids. Isn't it actually tall Yuko, who has come to rob the kids who work for him? Suddenly paralysed, his muscles stiff, Alam tries to escape to the high plateaus of Kandahar. He falls asleep, he is already dreaming. Someone very old, holding a long pipe between his hands, his head wreathed in a turban of smoke, tells him the story of the young man in his black marble palace who was turned to stone, from his toes up to his stomach. The brain mixes and stirs up masses of images. A thick salty liquid covers his face: it is the rotten blood of memory. He calls for help; his voice cuts across the wall of darkness in the distance. But Yuko has jumped on him and is crushing his throat. "Shut up! You want me to get caught?" The leaning face looks like the blade of a scythe in the half-light. Leave, go far away, to America, thinks Alam. One of his companions in the sewer at the station in Rome had had the time to give him a safe address before the roundup: *Alam Bridge* in fact, near the Eiffel

Tower. Can a bridge be an address? Yuko is pressing down on his chest with all his weight. The scythe swishes for a moment longer above his bed. "You want to escape, do you? Give me your dough and I'll tell you where to go, a squat near a housing estate, some friends told me about it…" Yuko seems to be sneering. "If you don't have any dosh, I even take medals, watches, gold teeth…" A monitor's footsteps hastens the intruder's departure. Alone in the night, with the energy of a condemned man, Alam pushes back the swaying gallows of sleep. But the images resurface all jumbled together, burning, fractured.

4

Well before the harvest, the dryness had scorched the poppy
flowers exposed to the One Hundred and Twenty Day wind that
blows incessantly from the Iranian plains. The salt dust bleached
the leaves and the fruit pods collided with a murmur of shells. "It's
like the sea!" says One Eyed Alam. Then, sadly, to his brother:
"One day, maybe, you'll see the sea." Their father, his face as gaunt
as the mountains he was contemplating, was standing facing the
wind. They could see the village, with its small, brand new mosque
in an arid recess, and the un-harvested fields along the protective
Gulbahar mountain range. Here and there traditional crops-wheat,
sorghum, barley, millet alternated in narrow plots wrested from
the stony ground with hoes and ploughs. Two bomber planes cut
through the circle of the horizon with the roar of a storm. Their
arrival had not the slightest effect on the exhausted features of the
farmers who had gathered before evening fell. They had just left
their poppies exposed to the fire of the skies and the torrential
blast: a few dozen hectares that barely brought in enough to feed
their families for half the year. The younger ones had little choice
but to sell themselves to the big farms in the irrigated lower valleys,
or to the vineyard and citrus fruit farmers who were short of day
labourers or shepherds. Within a few weeks, the Khan would come

to this part of the mountains, to inspect the raw opium harvest. He would arrive in his bullet-proof sedan, always preceded by a squad of body guards armed to the hilt. The Khan was a kind man; he never got angry and never allowed himself to bargain. His price included an approximate amount of compensation that the drug barons paid the farmers. To compensate their losses due to excessive rainfall, when the One Hundred and Twenty Day wind had dried up the plants, or when the local police, looking for a *baksheesh,* had amused themselves by uprooting a part of the harvest. Up in the mountains, the rebels paid no attention to a traffic they had themselves proscribed while they were in power, as long as the farmers under their control unquestioningly followed the Sharia. They visited the village after nightfall to collect provisions, or to reassert their authority, using whiplashes or Kalashnikovs if they had to. The poorest of the farmers sometimes allowed one of their boys to follow them into the mountains. They could hardly refuse. The insurgents descended from their hideouts at dusk or dawn, armed with assault rifles and rocket launchers. The new mosque, financed by Saudi Arabia, was to some extent their doing, proof of the good relationship between this Kandahar district's war chief and the generous investors in the Gulf.

An eye patch over his right eye, One Eyed Alam studied a world without relief or perspective. A large flat map on which he could place his own landmarks: there, in the accordion of the mountains the warlord, Ustad Muhib had stationed his men. He operated under the insurgent's banner; and everywhere else in the open, the plodding toil of a people made of clay and memory continued. One Eyed Alam would never endure the life his family lived, cloistered in bitter submission and austere pride. Here, death seeped out from every poppy pod. Between the mosque built by the petrol dealers and this edge of the desert, life was only interminable erosion, watched by the blind violence of the sky.

On the way home, One Eyed Alam picked up a stone that he pretended to throw at his brother. "Get away from me, the Unconscious!" he shouted. "I don't need a frightened puppy at my heels!" The child dodged the projectile and stopped in the yellow dust of the path, his arms hanging at his sides. The farmers all walked past him, the young and the old, some limping, others leaning on a stick, an exhausted cohort shrouded in dust. With just one wing, dusk covered the Gulbahar foothills. They heard the cry of a predatory eagle at the zenith, where the final glare of this day was concentrated. In the ash raised by their feet, the farmers in their greyish clothes were indistinguishable from the thorny bushes and the charred shrubs. Their shadows grew long enough to reach him, terrifying, like dead people being dragged along. Nothing about the muffled brutality of things amazed him. At his age, the whole world was like his father's house. In the oncoming night, once again the child returned in silence, following the old man and the nonchalant older brother who tripped over stones and with a leap pulled the last leaves off a skinny birch or an almond tree. The closely knit cubes of the shacks were already visible, giant dice or dominos on this forgotten step of the mountains.

At the farm, between the sagging ceilings and the gritty walls of the common room, he eats his chickpea and broad bean soup under the harsh gaze of the head of the household. At the corner of the table, One Eyed Alam sadly contemplates the murky depths of his plate. The women bustle about them uselessly. "What will become of us?" laments the unveiled mother with her grey braids. Ma'Rnina, the old relative brings the bread and the salt, without drawing undue attention to herself. Since her husband and two sons were summarily executed she exists less than ever, a family servant taken in during a moment of pious distraction. One by one, out of the corner of his eye, One Eyed Alam studies the only little brother who survived the childhood fevers, his trembling mother, beset by the thousand sorrows of renouncement, and this widow who has retreated to the depths of her being. And lastly, this man he hates so much, a slab fallen off the mountain, colder and more disdainful than a tomb, an ineradicable tree stump barring the desert.

Alam smiles into his sparse adolescent's beard. Soon he will be fifteen and all he had known would have been wars of invasion, the ones they recount and the ones that kill, the neighbouring Russians' wars or those of the Western powers. Who discusses civil war? The civilians like his father or these grazing farmers do not get involved in the battles. With wistful pride he remembers the episode that cost him his left eye, in a poppy field on the slopes where he was busy slitting the husk of the ripe fruit. A clash between a column of rebels and the regular troops had ended with him being hit in the face by a grenade shard. He was only about twelve at the time, but in the evening under his mother's compresses soaked in warm water, in the meanderings of the fever, a decision that tasted of departure crept into him. One day or another, when he could look his father in the eye without having to bow his head, he would leave the village to follow Commander Muhib and the insurgents. Children much younger than him were fighting in their ranks. Why should he suffer this miserable life amidst bleating goats and Sacrificers? Before they had destroyed the little school built by the Canadians at the far end of the small town, Alam dreamt of learning, of becoming a true *taleb*, not a rambling madrasa teacher; he was the best at reading and counting. One night the insurgents burnt down the school. Although he missed the lessons taught by the teacher who came from the town, he knew he would not be able to resist the desire to brandish a gun for long. In this land, the sheep skinner can only be an unwilling sheep. One Eyed Alam never missed an opportunity to court the rebels on guard duty. He dreamt of proving his worth one day to the war chief, the very one who had burnt down the school and chased away the teacher amidst general indifference. Reciting the Names is more than enough for farmers' children. *Allahou Akbar!* What else can one learn under the sky in this lonely place?

But his father got up from his chair in silence. Her head bent, his mother followed him into the alcove, behind the carpets that hung down like a screen. Ma'Rnina began to clear the table, humming an odd monotonous chant. Seated before his empty plate, the child would like someone to talk to him. The cats and the poultry in the courtyard enjoy talking to him. His older brother, who has turned away, displays his dead eye. They had explained it to him once and for all: it was his fault that Alam lost an eye. You should never lag behind when the mountain erupts.

The disgrace had begun on the day of his circumcision. *Get rid of the pagan's long hair* said the Prophet. The women had shaved him closely. Then the men had taken hold of him. A huge hand had turned his head away, while others restrained him as one would a sacrificial sheep; but he had caught a glimpse of the Sacrificer's blade gleaming between his thighs. Then he had fainted. He had passed out, to his father's great shame. The gathering of men muttered gravely. The women, who were soon informed, burst out laughing. He had regained consciousness a few minutes later in the bare arms of the women who washed corpses, duly circumcised and christened with a new nickname: the Unconscious. That very evening, determined to avert the dishonour, his father had thrust the handle of a pickaxe into his hands. He was ordered to go down into the ravine where the village's dirty water flowed, to kill the enormous rats that hid there. Although he had brought back half a dozen, their snouts dripping with blood, he could not get rid of the nickname. For the village and the universe, he would always be the Unconscious.

Unknown to him, this ordinary evening in the hollow of the mountains marked a transition. There was no one to hear it. Even the silence was filled with indifference. The war around him monitored every sigh. On his straw mattress, in a small corner of a room entirely occupied by his brother, his eyes followed a cockroach moving over the rope carpet placed directly on the beaten earth. A ray of moonlight lit its path. Outside, the tawny owl called with its trembling cry. One Eyed Alam was not asleep. Sitting on his bed, with its wooden frame held together by bits of wire, he grumbled about the vermin. Now and then he recited a fragment of a surah in the muezzin's shrill tone, or began to snap his fingers to the tune of *Yellow Submarine*. Secret dreams were his black pearl in the night. With a cockroach as his only companion, his young brother guessed that he had no place in his brother's wakeful agitation. Born in the shapeless disaster of wars he was stamped with the imprint of failed lives. But something in the solitude of the mountains cradled him and held him tight. By repeating simple gestures, like driving the goats and the ewes to the slopes covered in short fine grass, or slitting the poppy pods, he would manage to resemble the farmers closely enough. Over the years he would slip into the skin of one of them, obsessed merely by each day's survival and the call to prayer. Nonetheless, a dream gripped him, with its colourful cocks and bald moon. On the back of a cockroach wearing a petal, he was flying over the rippling multitude of small wounded skulls in the fields.

5

It was an ordinary morning. They had just finished weighing the dried resin before packing it in poppy leaves, watched by children who wondered whether this was something edible. The farmers had been warned of the Khan's imminent arrival one day this week. "When we will be capable of transforming the opium ourselves, we'll be rich", declared a young cultivator who owned the best land. The others noisily mocked his presumption. "And who will organise the transportation, the police maybe?" shot back a solid turbaned young man, collapsed against the shoulders of a yak. "Why not us?" retorted One Eyed Alam, with the wisdom of his fifteen young years. "There are more than enough weapons in the mountains". He was terribly proud of having spoken up in this gathering of adults. Who among them would dare cross the check-points and the borders, risk being racketed in Pakistan or being hanged in Iran. I would! declared Alam, inside himself. Me, I would challenge the Parsi's demon in order not to have to eat your mules' straw! But he bent his head under his father's gaze. Standing amidst his peers, his mind reduced to ashes by the thought of God, the old man was grimacing; his face looked as if it had been carved out of a bear's shoulder blade. How could this mummy who possessed only two or three basic reflexes and

who was filled with all the emptiness of the desert, have imagined
that his brood existed outside of the Law? This did not prevent
him from dealing with the Khan, the Dari who wore crocodile
skin shoes, despite the insurgents' warnings. One Eyed Alam was
in a position to know that Ustad Muhib, the war chief, was not
pleased that a dealer from the city of Kandahar, a close friend
of the local police, was encroaching upon his territory. During
a courtesy visit to the Imam, hadn't Commander Muhib asked
him personally to keep him apprised of the activity in the village?
In a way he was his secret agent, in exchange for a vague promise
of one of the beautiful guns, stolen some time ago from the
Soviets. Once, on the road to Gerestik and Pir Zaden, he had
stumbled upon the execution of a renegade, a former rebel who
had become a horticulturist. Shot at point blank range, his head
had exploded in a geyser of blood. He also remembered somewhat
uncomfortably, watching an adulterous woman and her lover
being lapidated at the gates of a small town to the East of the
Gulbahar mountains; a place famous for its copper mines and
deposits of precious stones. A crowd of scruffy men had suddenly
begun to throw large stones at the victims of this torture, who
were buried up to the waist, their heads covered by bags. The
rebels watched the proceedings with amused disdain, the butt of
their rifles proudly pressed against their hips.

"Here our crops are the only thing that matters !" announced
the father, decisively. Opium or sorghum flour, his other son did
not understand the importance of these calculations and these
weighing manoeuvres carried out with the application of a bomb
disposal squad. In reality, nothing seemed important to him apart
from the sorrowing attention his mother paid him when she was
not biting on her veil, crying, and the games, children his age
banished from school, played. He had to sort the wheat grain or

take the ewes out to pasture in the hills. The villagers made fun of him, even the girls too young to wear the veil, the youngest, whom the boys stared at intently so as to remember their beauty destined for secrecy. Despite the rats killed with the handle of the pickaxe, people openly made fun of the Unconscious. Most of the boys proudly disguised this intimate wound below their stomachs, ready to transform it into blind rage against adversity one day. Every one of them had felt their young male confidence reviled. Dogs, born out of their own flesh, they henceforth had to make people believe in their strength, but more than one trembled in their dreams under the Sacrificer's blade. Was it not after all the intention, to be cut off forever from women and their mysterious downfall? As for him, he had swooned with terror, like the lamb at the sacrificial celebration. They called him a girl; they threw dry poppy petals in his face. How could he guess that greater violence could exist?

This is what took place the day after the ritual weighing of the annual harvest, just before the cold season sets in. As usual, without further warning, as the day ended, the Khan and his militia arrived in their cars, preceded by a brigade of armed men on motorcycles. The dealers had left Kandahar individually to avoid attracting attention and had formed a convoy as they approached the village. The status quo with the local powers on both sides, insurgents and government police forces, did not preclude almost military precaution.

Once his men had taken up strategic positions, the Khan immediately went to meet the village spokesman. They knew his arrogance, his manner of adding a few wads of Afghanis from his pocket to the sums handed over by a paymaster with a long moustache, nicknamed Ala ad-Din. As clan leader, the Khan skilfully reconciled antagonism. Despite a few protests from the less well-off cultivators, everything was carried out with perfect civility, respecting the specific codes of the local farmers, former nomads from the Registan desert who had not forgotten their strong sense of independence. The Khan and the village elders were in perfect agreement about the manner in which the tasks were divided: the producers were responsible for harvesting the latex; it was up to the intermediaries to risk their lives. Tea was served on a covered terrace while they finished loading the goods into the boots of the vehicles. It was then that a warning shot sparked off a budding panic among the villagers. A mortar had been fired from the foothills. A muezzin's megaphone began to crackle. The insurgents were demanding their share of the negotiations. The leader ordered the dealers to lower their weapons. The Khan's intrusion into their district was a provocation. But the latter had no desire to enter into further negotiations. He signalled to his men to hasten their departure. This movement, visible from the heights, set off an intense round of firing. Machine guns and automatic weapons swept the facades and the dust of the roads, mowing down a dog or a child, here and there. The paymaster nicknamed Ala-ad-Din fell under a burst of fire. The Khan took charge of a rocket launcher that silenced the megaphone. His emboldened militia sprayed the foothills with varied projectiles. In response, the windows and roofs of the shacks were subjected to incessant gunfire. The rammed earth of the dividing walls crumbled a bit more with each volley. Hit with full force as the poultry clucked around them, two dealers wriggled oddly before collapsing. One of them, still alive, dragged himself along on his elbows towards an illusory shelter.

At the first explosions, One Eyed Alam and his brother had taken shelter under a cart full of straw. The apprentice sycophant bit his lips at the idea he may have been responsible for such chaos.

Beyond terror, his younger brother shivered, mesmerised by the action. He was appalled at the mad deployment of destructive energy that had such pathetic effect. The firearms burnt up kilos of powder. Empty cartridges were strewn over the beaten earth square, where only a wounded dog was still a target, while the stone of the low walls disintegrated in the rustle of a dune in the wind. Of course, the main idea was certainly to intimidate the adversary, to keep him away. The villagers had evaporated, going to ground in their shacks, leaving the goats and sheep free to wander. The animals were no more frightened by this firework display, than by a storm. In fact, they showed not the slightest interest in those that fell and rolled in the dust. A burst from a Kalashnikov stirred up the earth two metres from the cart. To forget the danger, the child focused his attention on the last jerks of the dying dog. Around its blood stained muzzle, the shouts and detonations took on a certain unreality. What if nothing really existed apart from trembling and glimmers, if men's words and gestures held no meaning, if the whole world were only the paralysis of a dying animal? One Eyed Alam tried to stop him as he extricated himself from under the cart to leap through an intense volley of bullets. He started dancing about under the hail of lead, as if to prove to himself that nothing was real, that death was playing with him, that nothing could happen to the Unconscious. Strangely, the firing stopped almost instantly on all sides. They saw the Khan and his militia run towards the vehicles and take off at full throttle, without provoking any further reaction from the rebels. The latter retreated towards the slopes soon afterwards, on their donkeys or on foot, awkwardly supporting the few wounded. When the surroundings were perfectly silent, one after the other, the stunned looking villagers emerged from their shelters. The square was cleared; the scattered rags were picked

up, as well as the huddled dog and a few chickens worth plucking.
A little girl who had been hit in the legs was taken home. In their
hurried departure the dealers had abandoned one of their men,
riddled with bullet holes. It was the paymaster with his handsome
moustache, the money collector, drained of his blood. One Eyed
Alam was the last to emerge from his hiding place. With the
greatest astonishment he had watched his brother's decapitated
chicken's farandole, convinced he would see him collapse at any
moment. That he could have survived unharmed, thrust him
into an incomprehensible rage; he was about to throw himself
upon him to beat him up when Ma'Rnina came out to call them,
barefoot, her face hollow with concern. "Quick!" she shouted.
"Your father has fallen down…"

With no other information, they thought he had been hit by
a stray bullet and lay drenched in his blood. The farmer was in
fact lying on the ground between the doorway of their dwelling
and a window that let in a drab ray of sunshine. Biting a corner of
her veil, their kneeling mother stammered out the timeless chant
of suffering. Mechanically, she dipped compresses in a saucepan,
then applied them to the old man's forehead. He was lying
stretched out like a slumbering caiman. The globes of his eyes
rolled in the pools of their orbits. The line of his lips was no wider
than a scalpel slit under the ridge of his nose. Yellowish, formed
only of angles and hollows, he looked like one of the lizard skin
masks that the trader's caravans sometimes brought back from
the Chinese borders. "Is he dead?" whispered the elder boy, in a
dull voice. "No! No! His eyes are moving", mumbled his brother,
terrified by the unfathomable virulence of these words.

The women asked for help. Ma'Rnina had grabbed the
farmer by the feet. "It's nothing", she says, "he will wake up.
Let's carry him to his bed". While One Eyed Alam staggered

under the weight of the inert trunk, the child responsible for the dry branch of an arm was surprised by a sudden desire to laugh that was intensified by his fear. Had his father fainted like a girl, him too? They laid him down in the alcove on the only feather mattress in the house. Apart from a tremor in an eyelid, there was no sign of life, but more than ever, a terrible severity emanated from the patriach's inert carcass. Fashioned by the law, he was his own statue. "Maybe it's an attack," says Ma'Rnina. "We should take him to the doctor". Thoughts drifted slowly like clouds over the wife's face, as she continued to busy herself with the compresses. If he died, what would happen to them? Alam was too young to take over from him. If he lived, how would they take care of him? The Khan's money was barely sufficient to pay the debts and buy food. On Ma'Rnina's orders, the two brothers ran off to fetch the Imam and the village chief. Both men sent them packing though; they had five wounded to deal with and an unknown corpse on their hands. Their unconscious father could wait.

It was only several hours later that a work horse was harnessed to the straw-laden cart to transport the old man and the little girl, wounded in the legs, to the nearest town. The children stayed behind alone in the subdued house. Ma'Rnina and their mother, both in full mourning, had chosen to accompany the farmer. Memory is full of distorted images illuminated by a distant fire.

At the age of seven years and nine months, on a calm night, the Unconscious surveyed his surroundings with a cat's cautious gaze. Everything was in its place, the pale walls riddled with bruises, a few crates that served as furniture, the dreamy evening light, and even the furtive snout of the mouse, poking out of its hole. A feeling of uneasy solemnity surrounds certain incomparable events, when a whiff of death replaces the hum of everyday life. Until then, his life had been divided between the sparse pastures, the poppy fields and his village that looked like unearthed ruins. As long as the rebels stayed holed up in their hideouts, the call of the muezzin and milking the ewes sufficed to structure his days.

Shortly after midnight, his forehead pressed against a splintered window pane, he studied a reflection of the moon diffracted on to the terraced roofs and the shadowy ramparts of the Gulbahar mountains. Pipistrelles flitted around the minaret topped by a dome encrusted with patterns shaped like arches and diadems. Neither the renewed calm of the place nor One Eyed Alam's peaceful snoring could reassure him. *The night of destiny is worth more than a thousand months,* says a surah, but he did not see any angels and he could barely count up to twenty-seven. He had to keep watch, his forehead against the window, hoping for a sign of salvation from the most absent of shadows.

At dawn, a white sun that gave off no rays rose over the mountains like a sea of milk.

6

It truly was a new life, in the thick of a crowd deprived of horizons. A town is an immense house shared by strangers. Everywhere under the low walls surrounding the buildings, there were carriages harnessed to mules, trucks, motorcycles that farted, salesmen on delivery tricycles or pushing carts through masses of porters, peddlers, watermelon and pomegranate stalls, people selling drinks or fritters, shoe polishers, all kinds of people looking for something and scrawny dogs. The street clamoured from daybreak onwards and each muezzin was noisier than a hundred cocks. Blue or black chadris, their hoods meshed with lace netting, contrasted sharply with the public cries from stalls that invaded the pavements: these towers of silence proceeded furtively amidst the unkempt crowd of barefoot men and children. Like daylight ghosts they slipped through secret stairways, going from one sign to another, along alleys encumbered with hammering craftsmen and fresh vegetable sellers, hairdressers and goldsmiths equipped with miniscule tools, crippled beggars whose only wealth was their stumps and small vendors selling single cigarettes or telephone cards. The roar of an US Air Force aeroplane crossing the sound barrier or the likely explosion of a mine in the distance, interrupted the gestures and glances for an instant. In the blink of an eye turned skywards the war resurfaced in everyone's memory. Then they immediately gave themselves up again to the secret laws of the crush, heads lowered in the vast tumult of intermingled destinies.

On the third floor of a brick building, the flat, sublet from one of the family's relatives, had no sanitation facilities and echoed as loudly with the sounds from the neighbours as from the loudspeakers of a nearby mosque. But apart from a crack in the wall at the end of the corridor, through which an old Sikh's beard sometimes made a furtive appearance, they were sheltered from curious eyes. In his role as the Unconscious, his mother's whining and Ma'Rnina's fussing no longer had much effect upon him and he had stopped begging for One Eyed Alam's attention. The latter used to leave at the muezzin's first call, to gather with the young men on mopeds at the gates of the community stadium.

In his isolation, he developed a sort of passion for the building's staircase, with its snake-like banister that vibrated from top to bottom at the slightest touch, and its hollowed out steps that shifted more than the huge wall drawers at the spice and semolina shops. At all hours and at varying speeds, the unknown kin of the neighbours went up and down. Few children deigned to greet him, he, the child of farmers, with his misshapen shoes and his antelope eyes. Everyone knew the new tenants survived on a sporadic income since the head of the family's aneurism.

Secluded in the corner of a lightless room in his invalid's armchair, his head bent over an abyss, the old man waited for someone to bathe and feed him. Paralysed and dumb, he exuded a heady smell of lard and poppy; a half-century of being immersed in the rustic world seemed to need to radiate from him. When he came back from the street or the staircase his youngest son approached him sometimes, to sit cross-legged at the old man's feet, watching him intently, like those forbidden stone statues.

He even spoke to him occasionally, very softly, from within his lips, from inside his brain. "Can you hear me, broken papa, its me, it's the Unconscious. Why are we here doing nothing? Who is looking after the goats and the sheep now? Why do you sit there immobile?" A drop of oil slipped from the old man's eyelid. His eyes never shone with anger any more. The strangeness of day was reflected through the cornea. The Unconscious was born of this sad statue and a fountain, in the hollow of the mountains, with the muezzin's call as his only promise. And here he is now, lost among men, between the bottomless wardrobe of the staircase and the screaming narrowness of the streets. Weary, he ends up returning to the obscurity of the landings. Two or three neighbours, among those who were the least overwhelmed by obligations related to the Sharia and housework, finally noticed his sharp cat's nose that spider webs stuck to sometimes. A young girl's voice thus fell from the lace porthole of a sort of diving suit made of unbleached blue fabric, smelling of orange blossom. "Oh! But you must be so bored all alone in the shadows! You should go to school like me ..." The voice was so clear and so cheerful. Not in the least used to anyone paying him the slightest attention, he was distraught the whole day. In fact nobody spoke to him. As a result, he was constantly on the look out for the blue chadri with its thousand reflections, as it went past every morning. The young girl lived on the second floor with her good mother, a war widow constantly busy with her washing, so he chose a fairly wide step on the first floor, in the corner, so that she took the time to stop. "Oh it's the staircase cat!" she liked to exclaim. Or even, when she was in a darker mood, "Do you know the way to paradise, little cat?" She found him so thin under his dark fur that one morning she came down earlier to invite him up. One Eyed Alam was leaving the house just then and shot them a disdainful look before disappearing: "Come to my place", she had sung out, Mama has heated a bowl of milk for you'. As he vehemently refused to go along with her, she burst out laughing: "Oh but what a wild little boy! Do you prefer crunching on mice?"

On the third floor, on the same landing as the family, lived a very ancient Sikh with his beautiful white silk turban. One day, departing from his usual reserve, the man handed him a slightly crumbled biscuit that had certainly been long forgotten at the bottom of a pocket. Baba Naka claimed he had lived in this building for centuries; his whole family had fled to Pakistan, the uncles, the sisters, the tribe of cousins and grand nephews. As an old bachelor who had taken refuge in his ancestor's faith, he feared no one. They could well chop off his nose; it would be one reason less for conceit. The old Sikh with his immaculate turban got into the habit of giving the thin inhabitant of the staircase a biscuit; the latter accepted the offering without a word of thanks, as if it were a ritual dedicated to silence. The old man's golden smile was as awe-inspiring as his solemn Billy goat's beard. For a long time their exchange was limited to this. One day, Ma'Rnina brought up a garbage collector who cleared the end of the corridor of a heap of dustbin bags full of scraps of sheets and clothes, the remainder of their former life. A glimmer lingered on in the wall, a deep reflection. Then through the crack the child glimpsed an enigmatic scene. Seated on a carpet at the centre of an empty room, Baba Naka sang voicelessly; to accompany his song he played a stringless lute, its bare body decorated with a rosette and its neck inlaid with mother of pearl. The only sound was the hum of a winter cricket. But such a sweet harmony filtered through this frail music that he was captivated. The Sikh invested his singing with a fervour that had no relation to the acoustic impact. The muezzin's metallic chant suddenly covered this insubstantial voice that seemed to have popped out of a picture. If the Earth were flat, as Ma'Rnina claimed, objects and creatures must also be flat. There was too much noise and too many gestures in this level world. Nonetheless, the old Sikh finally noticed a pair of eyes in the crack. He approached worriedly, without putting down his mutilated instrument. "I will have to buy a couple of litres of plaster", he said, before his young neighbour identified himself by a strangled laugh.

The next day or the day after, a terrible blast shattered some of the windows. As it happened every three weeks in one part of the town or another, a homemade bomb had gone off two streets away, in front of a finance ministry building that housed a police station. Terribly excited, One Eyed Alam was back fifteen minutes later, bringing news and rumours about the events outside. He had been able to see the burning car, the bodies of the passers by torn to shreds, the rutted front of the building and the policemen running in all directions. "People were shouting: it's Allah's punishment! They're all corrupt, like the people in the government; they steal from the poor and grow rich on international aid. This is God's punishment!" Ma'Rnina told him to be quiet. "Go off and work at the mine instead of spending your time with thugs!" Not in the least intimidated by the poor woman, Alam retorted to keep up appearances: "What thugs are you talking about? My friends study at the madrasa, they feed me, they take me to the stadium on their lovely motorbikes!" Ma'Rnina shrugged her shoulders and shaking a cloth out of the window, repeated wearily: "Go and work at the mine instead". One Eyed Alam turned gaily to his brother: "I heard the neighbour invited you to her place? How lucky you are! But tell me, is she really all that beautiful? Her mother tells everyone that such a beauty would honour Allah's paradise. You, you're a kid, she must have shown you her face ..."

Once the adolescent had left again, slamming the door, he felt an infinite sadness overwhelm him. The allusions the big boys made, their mischievous words, this avid curiosity about certain things that engulfed them, kindled a nameless distress within him. He would have liked to embrace the tender ochre of the sky above the roofs, to lie down naked and let the wind carry him off like a cloud into the secret of the azure, to die maybe.

The whole area was locked down within the quarter of an hour following the attack; reinforced by an army contingent the police inspected buildings, courtyards and shops. Baba Naka did not reply to his guests. They had pushed open his door that was never locked and were leaving now, spitting at the threshold. The old Sikh had not stopped singing in complete silence:

True. At the beginning He was
True. Through the ages He was
True. Today He is.

Through the crack, the mountain child repressed his laughter. The armed men who had stepped onto the old man's carpet were wearing hob nailed boots and a beetle's body armour; their gestures were brutal and they were shouting. Indifferent, Baba Naka remembered a time that had been far worse. When the insurgents were in charge and they forced Hindus and Sikhs to wear a sign on their chests, when they crushed any one effeminate with the bulldozer's mechanical shovel, when they destroyed sacred statues and libraries, when they cut off thieves' feet and hands, when they broke dancers' legs and all the musical instruments ...

The police and army withdrew empty handed from the invaded area. As a consolation, some of the police officers had collected a few handfuls of Afghanis from ill informed shopkeepers and intimidated individuals. In the evening, when One Eyed Alam returned home, his nervous joy had turned to melancholy. In the recess that served as their bedroom, under the bulb smudged with fly marks, he removed his patch and suddenly turned around. "Look at me!" he barked. "I'm horrible, aren't I?" The left orbit hollowed out with glistening scars did disfigure him of course, but it also revealed otherwise irreproachable features. This wounded head on a slim body caparisoned with muscles lent him a cursed, savage air, enhanced by his excess energy. "Admit it then! If she were to see me, she would scream in terror!" Alam replaced his patch and leaned against the window. After this admission of weakness, he started bragging. "So!", he continued, "The Malalaï, is she as beautiful as her old bag of a mother claims? I wonder how she can bother wasting her time on a little mountain monkey like you!"

At night, the smell of lard and poppy emanating from the paralytic filled the apartment. Lying on a cover stuffed with old, cut up clothes, near his older brother who tossed and turned on his mattress, the child wondered what fever was making him moan and shift about unceasingly.

Yes, Malalaï was beautiful, so much more than her mother, the proud widow kept proclaiming. The first time, distrustful of any kind of graciousness, he had refused to go along with her. The next morning, it took him a long time before he was finally willing to taste the steaming bowl of milk before him. Almost immediately, as is the custom within the family and in front of children, the young girl undid the embroidered cap and then extricated herself from the sort of camel's tent covering her. For the Unconscious, this was the maddest awakening. At that very second, he felt as if he

were ageless. Beside life's meagre objects the heavens had bestowed
a gift upon him. The widow, slumped in a Formica chair, smiled
blissfully at this sunrise. He had never experienced anything as
miraculous. A finger of light originated at the tip of his hair and
ran right through him, burning him even more sweetly than the
rustle of the poppy flowers in the summer wind. Are there words
for beauty? Malalaï's face was a slow illumination, a secret that
reveals itself over and over, like the fiery horizon, contemplated
from a shady spot at the top of the pastures.

His older brother had not even needed to see her to fall in
love with her. A fragrance and a reputation had sufficed for him.
Every evening, his lone eye gazed at a prohibited image. A dream
gnawed away at him. He continued to question the nameless
child with the same vehemence: "Have you seen her? Have your
little monkey's eyes glimpsed Paradise? Tell me! Tell me what is
under the veil!"

7

The offices of the Holding Centre for Minors in Irregular Situations had been broken into and looted during the first night of December. The police detectives had no difficulty in identifying the perpetrators. Yuko's fate as the instigator of the crime was soon to be settled. They were going to take him away to an administrative detention centre for foreigners, before deciding on his level of responsibility in this act.

As they were being questioned, he and Alam found themselves momentarily on the same bench in the hallway near the offices, watched by a sleepy policeman who was not very vigilant. "They're going to send me to prison", says Yuko, who is handcuffed. "I'll escape though. You, you're in no danger, you're just a kid, and anyway, you haven't done anything". Alam is surprised at this unexpected indulgence from this amateur villain. His concerned manner and his breathless speech seem to indicate that the dormitory's ringleader is scared to death. Yuko tries to clutch at a familiar face, any one will do. From the depths of his agitation, helpless, he would like to cling to the slightest ersatz of affinity. "I know a good squat!" he whispers abruptly as they take him away. "It's in Bobigny, the brick factory dead end, behind the old cemetery ..." Two policemen arrive to take delivery of the young delinquent. Deathly pale, Yuko turns back again towards the last familiar face. "Don't forget, Bobigny, the brick factory! We'll meet there, huh?"

Cleared of suspicion thanks to Diwani's statement, Alam returns to the literacy class. What little he had been able to learn earlier in the Pashto language is no longer of any use to him. Everywhere he goes he is treated like a dunce, just like Diwani, the pretty Tutsi who nonetheless knows three idioms from the Great Lakes region. The skills he had accumulated on his own in the mountains with his goats and ewes, were mocked by the city dwellers. The little knowledge he went on to assimilate later at the public school in a small mining town meant nothing to the warlord's followers concealed in the mountains and valleys. It was like owning sand in a desert. In fact, he no longer knows anything. The waters of forgetfulness have run for so long over his hands and his face.

Today, to keep him occupied, the teachers explain French grammar, the past tense and the past perfect. What kind of hidden perfection is it? As for the future, he has understood, it is what will inevitably happen.

In the garden with its portcullis covered in barbed wire, the lawns and the flowerbeds of winter roses are stiff with ice. The branches of the trees seem to be made of crystal. A couple of magpies squabble on the awning of a disused dovecote where the lens of a surveillance camera gleams. Silhouettes are visible on the other side, at the bottom of a steep path. They come and go, leaning into the wind on a freezing avenue. Beyond a white line of buildings, the horizon bristles with chimney pots and cranes. His arms pressed against his body, clutching the empty copper gun casing and his emerald in his pockets, he tramples the slippery grass. Over there on the tar of the criss-crossed roads, articulated lorries drive past at great speed. He does not see any beggars on the pavements, nor shoe shiners or cigarette sellers, not one of the street characters whom he could ask why clouds are sometimes shaped like a woman's mouth, or how much a lost life could be worth on the black market. It is an empty world, with neither muezzin nor crouching camels, nor neighbour with a goat's beard. Lanes run between identical red brick pavilions with white plaster joints. A ceramic cat, its tail in the air, stands out on a tiled roof. Two live doves flap their wings as they fly off a television aerial to lose themselves high in the greyness.

On this side of the garden, an old layer of stone covers or replaces the outer fencing. Badly maintained, flanked by ivy columns, it is collapsing in places. Walls and mountains are less of a deterrent than electrified clearways, he had realised that for himself at the borders. Behind a holly and thuja bush he has crept into, the wall can be climbed as easily as a rockslide on a goat path. Getting down again is more difficult though, especially when you are wearing soldier's gear. Incidentally, dreams of falling forever come back to him. His hands are free though. He is in the street.

Now he runs over the tarmac, between two trucks travelling at breakneck speed. A breath of deliverance carries him through the exhaust pipe fumes. On the other side of the avenue, wary, he decides to follow one of the lanes that run uphill. A dull hum replaces the sustained throbbing of the motorway access roads. He passes rows of sleeping gardens and shuttered windows; here and there curtains part to reveal a face emerging from the shadows or a dreaming dog's muzzle. An ancient garage with its nocturnal depths emits a smell of fire. Whiffs of lime and freshly dug earth announce a neighbouring worksite. Where can he escape to on a winter Sunday, in the stupor of the suburbs? Another avenue

cuts through the suburban houses. To the West, where a low
sun pushes through, there are buildings and thick smoke; to the
East, the sky is broken by a flimsy jumble of scaffolding and steel
stakes. He feels as if he has returned to the interrupted path of
a thousand jolts through towns and countryside. But where can
he go in a closed world where only wastelands are abandoned? A
large grey cat jumps off a pillar next to a gate; it approaches him,
meows and runs off as soon as he bends down. Either real or made
of enamelled bisque, how many cats does one meet in a lifetime?
He remembers a story about travellers. A blind man dug his stick
into the ground and set off with a musician buddy to discover the
universe. Wherever they went, they were welcomed with open
arms; they were offered an abundance of food and a good bed
to sleep in. In exchange, the musician lulled the dusk with his
nostalgic songs. In each land, the blind man listened as people
talked, he imagined their lives. Back at home ten years later,
having learnt nothing, he asked his buddy to describe the journey
to him. Nobody answered, just the wind and the birdsong. He
realised then he had travelled alone. Had he ever gone any further
than where he had planted his cane?

Here comes a bus that luckily, stops just in front of him.
Travelling towards the smoke, the vehicle goes through a tunnel
and crosses blackened bridges. Slumped dully in their seats the
passengers dolefully watch the young illegal boy travelling without
a ticket. It was months ago now, near an Italian station, that he
and the others had had extricated themselves from a hiding place
at the back of an articulated lorry. Then, a boy with a Persian
accent that sounded Pashtu had soon taken charge of them after
a desperate race to escape the security guards and their dogs. In
exchange for a pittance, they had been promised a shelter and
something to eat. That was how he had found himself in the station

basement, with a few tins of food in his bag, in the company of about twenty kids aged between ten and fifteen. Nights and days of walking through the mountains, and how many more confined inside truck trailers and the baggage hold of a cargo ship, to end up in the depths of a sewer. 'You're safe here for the moment' the other refugees had told them, the adults who willingly allowed them to occupy the last water pipe basement. Tormented by the vermin, suffering from rat bites, all of them had been captured by the police several weeks later. A horde of Italian *Carabinieri* had cordoned off the manholes and all the exits around the station, to catch the children. Only he had managed to escape the roundup by clinging the whole night to the flying buttresses of a low gallery, submerged in filthy water. He was used to hiding and to killing field mice. In the mountains and the high plateaus of Kandahar, life is a permanent ambush. There, you swallow your tears in the shadow of corpses. The sewer kids were not used to it. With money earned by different means in Kabul, at the end of a year or two, the smartest of the tens of thousands of street children could finally pay the carpet and citrus fruit transporters who travelled to Daki or Istanbul, the lowest price for the journey. Other escorts in the network would take charge of them from there, sending them on by sea or air, if the money or their life had not been stolen before that.

Exhausted, Alam sat down on a bench in a square at the Porte de Bagnolet. People hurry through it in order to avoid the crowds at the crossroads. His toes and the tips of his ears are pinched by the cold. He has forgotten his cap and other possessions in the dormitory at the Centre. In reality, even thirty seconds before he discovered the way out, the thought of escape had not crossed his mind. Not so soon, without even taking his bag, or saying goodbye to Diwani. At the end of the square there is a swing. He gives in to the temptation, as there is no policeman's cap in sight. Children's games fill him with melancholy. The swing whines and the trees dance. A dirty man, his face the colour of wine, comes over and shakes the dead branches of his arms above him. He is not frightened of the man; only the sound of axles scares him, monotonous like the wheel of a nomad's cart in the Registan desert. "Death to foreigners, gypsies, Arabs", spews out the drunkard. He twists his body strangely, suddenly bursts out laughing and grimaces. His vacant stare is that of a madman. Alam thinks of the madmen from the high plateaus, those who have escaped an attempt on their life, those who watched as their house burnt down, their daughters were raped, as fathers or sons were decapitated. "Give me some bread", he says jumping off his perch. The dumbfounded man has fallen silent. He spins around looking for his head. Walking like a robot he finally runs towards a bench and brings back a plastic bag. The sandwich he shares leaks ketchup and mustard. By the time they have finished chewing on this bit of stale bread together, the man with black hands has calmed down completely. A smile spreads the fans of wrinkles at the corners of his eyes and his lips. "I am looking for Alam bridge", the child ventures, just in case. "You mean Alma Bridge? Its easy, you follow the Seine up to the Eiffel Tower and when you see a clown standing in the middle of the wine tanker boats that carry tourists and porpoises..."

The faces in the town drift past like clouds. Along the embankments near Notre-Dame a few hours later, the barges passing under the cast iron archway of the Pont-au-Double absorb him enough to banish his loneliness. Boats, he had never seen any before leaving the high plateaus; the rivers there are torrential and the sea is only a word. A dark-haired woman at the prow of a launch, her dress sticking to her and her hair flying in the wind, waves at him lazily.

And if everything were to stop all of a sudden, if the river stopped flowing and identical clouds paved the sky forever? The woman continues waving. Would she be carved out of wood and painted? But the launch disappears under the archway. The world comes to life again. Alam inhales the freezing air. Alive or dead he has to keep following the current, like the empty bottles and broken branches floating along.

8

The rain ruffles the murky, stagnant waters of the Saint-Martin Canal. On their way back from Boulevard de Ménilmontant, between the third lock and the Villette tank, Zar Gul and Tahar walk back towards the camp loaded with a crate of vegetables and a bag of fruit they have scrounged amidst the debris of the Belville market. With one hand Tahar holds a scrap of a work site tarpaulin over his head to protect himself. He is barely listening to his compatriot who, for the hundredth time, is telling him how they can reach London on a ferry from Cherbourg or Ouistreham, without going through Calais. Tahar is constantly amazed that he had been able to overcome so many obstacles to find himself in Paris, with no one to turn to for help. Between Kabul and Turkey, there were still ways of helping tomorrows to dawn. Here, there no longer seems to be a way out of misery. With no money or documents, one can just about survive. But the freezing rain and strangers' eyes fall relentlessly upon you. The custom here is to charge for the discomfort of pity, between two police raids and the threat of deportation.

The camp is tucked away under the small arches behind the lock, in the opening to the reservoir. Far from the busier quays, almost hidden from sight, they are not disturbed for the moment. Until the security services decide to carry out the next raid. When night falls, with the Villette rotunda and the illuminated pleasure boats, you could almost believe you were on the Bosphorus.

The two men have set down today's harvest, overripe fruit, and vegetables, gleaned from the heaps of crates after the stallholders had left. Gathered around a modest fire contained by paving stones and sewer plates, about a dozen refugees, most of them young, are crouching or leaning forwards, seeking answers to their future in the flames. Ozur, not yet forty, is the oldest. He busies himself separating the really overripe tomatoes before they rot. His nose in the crate, he congratulates the newcomers for their almost intact oranges. A clipped beard reveals more than it hides of the wide scar across his face. His fingers handle the fruit as delicately as they used to tackle the Soviet mines or the home-made bombs planted by Pakistani terrorists in his Panjshir valley. He had become a teacher for a while in the Kabul region after Commander Massud's death, so he speaks the language of the French civil servants as well as he does Tadjik. He also knows the 'Code for the entry and residence of foreigners and asylum seekers', guaranteed by the Constitution and the Geneva Convention of July 1951, by heart. The former bomb disposal expert reels off articles 13 and 14 of the Universal Declaration of Human Rights to counter the obstinate critics who work for the administration. He recites them like a traditional poem, never making the slightest mistake: *Everyone has the right to freedom of movement and residence within the borders of each state. Everyone has the right to leave any country, including his own, and to return to his country. Everyone has the right to seek and to enjoy in other countries asylum from persecution.* More than once, for his friends and himself, he has approached the Cimade* or the French Office for the Protection of Refugees and Stateless People, and has even sent a letter by registered post to the United Nations High Commission for Refugees, with its headquarters in Geneva. Ozur, however, is tired of the journey. One sets out discouraged, as a coward or a hero, with the illusion of a different life ahead, but there is no way out. Exile is a prison.

As the day runs out, a dark wind falls from the sky and the rain turns to snow. Zar Gul and Tahar split the old wooden pallets hauled out of the rubble skip of a neighbouring work site. The flames light up the faces. "Where have you come from, you?" shouts Ozur, as he catches sight of the child crouching at the centre of the group, his filthy hands stretched towards the fire. "I'm hungry", replies Alam in Pashtu. The others exchange looks, intrigued. Tahar hands the child a grilled corncob. "We're all Tajiks and Hazaras here. There's also an Uzbek in the tent, who's at death's door. Where do you come from, then?" But the child does not answer. He devours the corn, smiling. Ozur begins to laugh. "Don't be frightened of the little Taliban!" The others follow his lead noisily, reminded of earlier joys. The snow flies over the darkened waters of the canal. It swirls about above the live embers that Zar Gul is tending, curbing them between the cobblestones. "I worked in Kandahar", he murmurs, contemplating the sparkling spirit that seems to be fighting the army of snowflakes. "I was employed as a baggage handler at the airport..." Ozur points to the snow with a sweeping gesture. "You know the saying: "Whoever controls Kandahar controls Kabul! It's the President's clique and the opium dealers who decide...""

*The Cimade is a French NGO working with displaced people. It was founded at the end of WWII by French Protestant student groups.

It is far too cold to ponder the question. People nod their heads around the low flames. Each of them can make what they want of these words.

"Where do you come from?" repeats the Tajik. In French this time, Alam says he slept under Alam or Alma Bridge, that there were only Poles or Ukrainians there. Nobody would allow him to come close. They shouted to him: "Go beg on the boulevards, dirty gypsy!" So for the last two days he has been looking for his compatriots, along the Seine and the canal. "Looking for whom?" sniggers Tahar. "Pashtuns? There aren't any here. There are no kids either. Those of your age, we see them at Jaurès or Stalingrad*, under the elevated metro".

His hands stuffed into his sleeves to keep them warm, Ozur thinks he remembers an article of the old Constitution that dates back to the Communist period: 'All Afghani subjects, without restriction of race, nationality or tribal origin, language, gender, place of residence, religion, education, kinship, wealth and social rank, have equal rights and duties'. The circle of faces listens with amused astonishment. "Equality is for the rich," says Tahar. "Where we lived, there were only blood feuds, goats and the Sharia!". An ambulance or police siren breaks their concentration. Uniformed squads from the prefecture could appear at any moment. Under Alma Bridge the other week, most of them had been able to decamp in time, by the steps. The dawdlers immediately find themselves at an administrative detention centre in Vincennes or elsewhere. Once they have been sent back to where they came from on a special charter flight, they can only fear for their lives. Neither those in the government nor the insurgents have any sympathy for defectors. Back home, they are seen only as traitors

*Names of metro stations in Paris.

or spies. "The kid can't stay with us!" declares one of the Tajiks, wrapped in a survival blanket. The others agree or remain silent. "He's right," says Ozur. "We're not allowed to. Tonight the kid will sleep in the tent, with the Uzbek. And tomorrow, God will take care of him..."

The shadow of sleep carries the breath of death. It is a waking dream. He is walking over pebbles. Eagles are watching for the slightest tremor in the wormwood. Jackals slink around the ruins. Dislocated, grotesque in their puppet's awkwardness, corpses jest as they lie across the paths. They stick out their tongues; black blood spews out as they laugh silently. Alam trembles in the tent; he fights unconsciousness. Being awake is like the dream he has every night. A few centimetres away, burning with fever, the sick Uzbek gasps. He is thirsty; he does not want them to make him better. He would rather die than return to Kabul. His father was loyal to Massud. A grenade destroyed the family, the brothers and the little sisters. He refuses to be handed over to the killers. Alam shifts away from his burning heat. The smell of a burst abscess makes him gag. The allusion to an impending death heightens the dizziness around him. A thousand flies hiss against his face. The insurgents like chopping off hands. Bomber planes are not selective. All the enemies aspire to the strange peace that inhabits the dead. Daggers knit a carpet of guts. Why do people who have been machine-gunned lose their shoes? Bodies with twisted springs, with boa's eyes, cling to the last image: the lost shoe that no mother claims. The Uzbek utters a dull cry beside his ear. In his fever, he sees the past floating by, a skinny cat on the prayer mat, the cavernous mouth of an old smiling woman. He gestures weakly against the meanders of the delirium. Like a dead branch his arm falls onto the chest of the child who is alarmed by the gasping and the war. Paris is not so distant from the bombarded roads. Feeling his way, he wanders in the mined mists of time. A refrain beats against his temples. How can he get rid of his brother's still warm body? He would like to push away the embrace before the jackals return. With a jerk, Alam frees himself. He puts on his shoes, feeling his way in the dark, buttons up his anorak and creeps out of the shelter.

The fire has gone out. Everyone is asleep under the tarpaulin sheets. An ice moon is reflected in the broken windows of the canal.

With no landmarks, the ravines of the streets go by, identical. The doors and windows, the inhabited storefronts offer no shelter. The snow beneath the streetlights quivers like poppy flowers in the night wind. What occurs between two desperate escapes heightens his premonition. No one is waiting for him in the city. Every day is a freshly laid trap. With a family of dwarves he picks up an unenthusiastic hand-out in the corridors of the metro. But the children's shepherd soon chases off the intruder. On the other bank of the river, in the middle of a garden, he accepts the biscuits offered him by a very old lady surrounded by pigeons. In a concealed alley watched over by statues, a hunted man passes him by, his lips covered in drool, his open coat revealing a strip of flesh. Women burst out laughing a little further on. They point at the unbuttoned sight between the marble Venuses. Yet again, evening descends to put an end to this foolishness. It is time for him to make his nest of rags and shadows. He has to choose between the worksite shed, the unlocked car parked in a dark corner, or the entresol of a building stairway.

Amidst the crowd of immobile vagabonds at the entrances to the metro stations, in basements and hallways leading to supermarkets, he sometimes finds a way to rest. A fat woman concealing a new born baby in her layers of dresses and fur-lined

coats, allows him a whole night of her warmth. Against his cheek
the baby sucks on an enormous breast while above, the mother
crunches endlessly on cornflakes, crisps and bananas. Far from
the brutality of the open air, the newborn snatches like a fish at
this milk from the depths. Nestled against the other breast, the
Unconscious dozes, satiated with the sap of organs.

Under the elevated metro at La Chapelle the following
night, amidst the fabric of the tents marked with the initials of
Medecins du Monde, the immigrants from the East European
countries pretend not to notice him. Children are unlucky for
the homeless. They do however discreetly leave him a peaceful
corner. When in the early hours of the morning two drunks break
some glass and get into a fight, he does up his anorak and steals
away towards the open train tracks of the station. He does not
notice the illegal children of his age nestled under some boxes a
few dozen metres away. After hours of fishing for change around
the departing trains and a hare's race under the compartments to
escape the railway police, he skims along the windows of shops
selling shoes or sports clothing on boulevard Poissonière. Ragged,
exhausted, he feels that his escape is likely to come to an abrupt
end. He is increasingly the target of searching looks. Young or old,
when one lives in the street, the most important thing is to make
a good impression. In Kabul he was left more or less to himself, he
and the horde of street orphans; he could even work sometimes,
washing windscreens or selling cigarettes. Here he is hunted. Since
his shoes have started leaking, every uniform he passes yells at
him. But the lighted windows absorb him, like privileged homes
where only chosen parts of the anatomy are allowed to live, feet
and women's chests, heads with wigs. A man wearing a tie and a
raincoat approaches him; he has been following invisibly at his
heels for a long while. His perfectly combed hair and the silver

circles around the lenses of his glasses contrast with a sad carp's mouth. On the defensive, Alam notices his eyes with their liquid transparency under the glare. "Come home with me, I'm not a policeman, I won't harm you," whispers the individual, bending sideways. He indubitably belongs to the main species, the kind that has access to houses and cars, to restaurants, to all the refuges abundance provides. Whenever one of the innumerable owners of the town speaks to him, it is usually to chase him off or lecture him, and on occasion he can negotiate an indulgent euro. Smiling like an old lady, this one displays a bunch of keys. Alam follows him at a distance as far as the rue de la Lune. He crept along behind him up a beautiful staircase, smelling of polish and dead mice.

The door closed on a stuffiness tinged with English tobacco. Blood coloured curtains at the window reveal a series of zinc roofs planted with aerials and a Chinese cemetery of chimney pots. Painted figurines set out by the hundreds on furniture and shelves; lead soldiers organised in battalions, cavalry, heavy artillery, foot soldiers on a campaign, make the child wary. Does one maintain such a large army if one is not going to war? Hiding in his house, maybe this strange man is expecting a tiny enemy to creep in through the keyhole. The idea would almost be amusing, as he remembers a goat's goatee shaking like a cat's tail in the crack of a wall. Memory has its chosen ones and its ambassadors. One of the old Sikh's interminable stories comes back to him. Azri Svara, the monstrous snake with more horns than a tree, black venom spitter born of the mountains, is finally vanquished by Keresaspa, the audacious masked dwarf. The latter however sinks into a profound state of lethargy induced by three drops of poison the dying snake spat at him. Between mount Damavand and the Pishgaman plains, the whole region where these battles took place was then struck by a terrible evil spell. This is how the armies sent by the King of Afghanistan, to conquer India, found themselves petrified like the dark rock. Only the masked hero's awakening had the power to return them to their belligerent life. The dwarf, however was in a deep sleep in the middle of the mountains, and his dream eternally perpetuated his battle with the horned snake... What this story meant, Alam had not the slightest idea. In fact, he can hardly remember the old Sikh with his immaculate turban.

"I was a soldier," the stranger suddenly declares, less to justify his passion for the miniatures, than to awaken his guest from his torpor. A glimmer of childish joy flits over his face, quickly erased by a veil of wrinkles. Looking concerned he opens wardrobes, gathers up some clothes and finally rushes into the bathroom. The sound of running water covers his voice. Still distrustful, the child hears him humming. The man emerges in his shirtsleeves, slippers on his feet. "I've got some clothes ready for you, they were mine, they're almost new, you should have a bath now..." Puzzled, Alam seizes the opportunity. Once he has lowered the latch of the door, he watches the grey water swirl away down the plughole. When he has finished his bath, dressed in the manner of rich kids from an earlier time, he stares unflinchingly at his host. Embarrassed, the latter hurries to take a chicken and some tubs of yoghurt out of the fridge. He slices the bread then butters it with impish delight. "Sit down and eat. I only want to see you happy..." The man sits down facing the divan, some distance from the child. Casually, with no warning, he grabs an old pistol that had been hidden under a folded newspaper all this time. It is a MAC 50, semi automatic, French army issue. A cloth in his hand, he busies himself immediately taking apart the breech and the firing pin with precise gestures.

He counts and recounts the nine cartridges in the magazine like an orant telling his rosary. "Don't be frightened, he says, it's only a toy from when I was young, when I was in active service". As he devours a chicken thigh, Alam does not take his eyes off the 9mm. Up there, in the Kandahar mountains, there were more weapons than sheep. Kalashnikovs and machine guns abandoned by the defeated Russians, American assault rifles, entire crates of them distributed to the warlords, heavy weapons transported in separate pieces by camel caravans coming from Pakistan. "Lieutenant Pierrot reporting!" the seated man shouts, giggling. "Don't worry, I was thinking about things," he adds in a thin voice, after snapping the magazine into place.

Alam falls asleep under the retired soldier's unwavering gaze. The only dream that inhabits him is a vague impression of wandering through the night surrounded by the uninterrupted sound of metal being dragged along the ground. He wakes up on the divan. Opposite him, between two wooden beams that form the edges of a screen of varnished bricks, an ivory Christ, as naked as an old tooth, is nailed to a large wooden crucifix. He has never slept so peacefully. Dressed in new clothes, his fetishes in his pockets, he just has to put on his run down shoes and slip on his anorak. The pistol is still lying on the low table. The man has not stirred from his seat, he looks downcast, his lips tremble, "Thank you," is all he says. "Thank you for trusting me."

It is as he is going down the stairs that, without thinking about it, he makes the association between the image of the wall and the cross and the memory of Yuko handcuffed. "The brick factory dead end in Bobigny, behind the cemetery," the adolescent had whispered before two deaf and dumb policemen led him out of the Centre.

On the ground floor, between a large mirror and the glass doors of the concierge's lodge, a long-haired cat stops him with a friendly pirouette. He is confident too. The lovely animal approaches him and speaks in an eternal voice. Only cats and donkeys speak the same language everywhere.

9

The thunderous erruptions of the American forces' F-16 and F-18 fighter planes and B-1 bombers shook the hoary tree of the staircase and all the doors on the landings. A series of explosions echoed almost secretly quite far from the town. Late into the evening, long after this new storm, he had remained seated on a step, hoping One Eyed Alam would return. He had left in a rage to join his stadium acolytes, because of a rebuke uttered by Ma'Rnina. When a long inarticulate scream woke the whole building. The first to reach there, he did not at first comprehend the scene. Ma'Rnina and his whimpering mother, her face destroyed by the onrush of age, were bending vigorously over the paralytic, shaking and pecking at him like two magpies fighting over a lizard. Were they exacting revenge for the life of sacrifice they had lived? He pushed his way between them protectively. The old man's indifferent gaze was focused on a wall in the distance. All the cracks, splits, and defects had rearranged themselves harmoniously over this face that suddenly seemed to him to be complete, miraculously fulfilled. He stroked the hand clutching the chair's moveable arm and murmured the final word that the two women had been avoiding for a while with their exhortations. They immediately fell silent, and looked down at the child with horror, as if he had just insulted his father. "He is dead" repeated the Unconscious feebly, without removing his hand from the root of nerves and bones hooked around the aluminium support. The weight of destiny had caught up with them; Ma'Rnina was the first to find the customary words and gestures.

Back from the stadium, when One Eyed Alam entered the apartment, he was struck by this late gathering of neighbours around his crying mother. In the first instant he recognised Malalaï's silhouette. She was wearing only a veil that revealed a bit of her face, up to the wing of her nose and the corner of her lips. The shock he felt turned to fear at the incongruous sight of a body, all wrapped in white, lying on the floor, and his young brother praying. "Your father is dead and it's your fault!" Ma'Rnina spat dryly at him.

The very next day the deceased was buried, naked and embalmed, in a large sheet tied according to the precepts. The Imam pronounced his blessings in due form; in accordance with custom he announced the widow's civil death and the duties that fell to the children. One Eyed Alam abruptly repented. He shaved his head and cried for days and nights. He was seen performing the five prayers with dedicated energy, as if he were folding and ironing washing. Then he disappeared again one morning. Everyone imagined the crisis of mourning over; he returned that very evening, exhausted, his face black with dirt and he went to bed without saying a word. At dawn, exactly like the previous day, he left home to return before nightfall, just as tired and filthy. They had the impression he had taken a job at the copper mine. From then on, at the end of every week, he handed over a large proportion of his pay to Ma'Rnina, the only one capable of managing a budget. The remainder served to repay the loan for the moped that took him to the mine, a good ten kilometres away. One Eyed Alam's transformation was brought about by two inseparable causes: remorse and the cataclysm of love. As much as the paralytic's sudden death, the surreptitious vision of the young neighbour had struck him like a bolt of lightning. In the evening, he no longer asked his brother, with his young arrogant male curiosity, how beautiful the neighbour was, what shape her mouth was, what was the texture of her skin, whether she had breasts under the caparison of her veil. Broken by this deepest test, One Eyed Alam only questioned the silence of the night. The persecution of the overseers, the acrid dust and the din of the drilling turbines, the jackhammers and the skips squealing on the tracks drained him of all strength, so much so that Ma'Rnina had to serve him his bowl of broad bean soup in bed. The ore of dreams glimmered for a few instants in the blind thickness of sleep; Malalalaï was smiling at him, her face so bare that he trembled with shame and pleasure. She accepted him only through this act that opened up new horizons. There was no longer anyone to stand between them, the fathers had died and their mothers were totally crazy, nothing but a flight of stairs separated them and arms outstretched, staggering, he tried to reach her landing. In addition he saw her through the doors and the walls, so utterly beautiful that life or death no longer held any meaning. His only goal was to attain her; everything was concentrated in a single instant, the one that would obliterate the distance between her and him. Moaning and drenched in sweat he emerged from sleep with no memories. He got up quickly and shot an uncertain look at his young bother's cool neck, as he lay curled up. He prayed as the muezzin's call rang out, ready to set off again for the copper mines. With a wave of euphoria he thought of the moments of respite he would enjoy, racing against the wind on his new moped with its shiny chrome trimmings.

But the Unconscious was not asleep. Since the funeral, he was also experiencing exquisite heartbreak. One Eyed Alam's mad love only exacerbated his own devotion to Malalaï. Nonetheless, he was not jealous. He could well understand that people were driven to madness by their love for her. A few metres away, behind these walls a miracle of life existed, a creature of light compelled by the barbarian mourning of this world to hide away. He was the only one who could gaze upon her at will. Malalaï was the warm milk of his eyes; she received him almost naked in her long tunic, with its tight neck and wrists. Her migratory bird's neck, her hands like sugar, her delicate ankles that quivered with every step, all the delights no one else could see. He was the only one entitled to the perfumes and the jewellery, the veiled breast, the concealed leg. Malalaï enjoyed joking and laughing. Her lips curled upwards then, her hair with its blue highlights fell over her neck and a spring of joy flowed unannounced. Before laughing shyly himself, he had almost been offended. Her beauty abandoned itself without the outrageous arrogance of young schoolgirls. She revelled in it with coquettish indifference, like a Persian cat in languid hands. On rare occasions, on her return from the State high school she allowed the staircase child in and enjoyed reading to him. Seated nearby, embroidering the sleeves of a chadri, the illiterate mother looked on worriedly as Malalaï plucked poems out of a song book compiled by the famous Majrouh who was assassinated at the end of the first war, well before she was born: *When you return torn by the guns of the night, I will stitch your skin together with my kisses, O my sun. Or I will blow on your dust after midnight, my beloved ...* Attentive, her mother nodded her head. Not so long ago, the man or woman who dared read things like this would have risked lapidation. Was that in another century? She had lost her husband ten years before, during the battles against the insurgents who were in power at the time. Malalaï's father was a well-respected man who could recite the one hundred- and- four surah by heart and refused to accept the criminal interpretations of the Sharia. Unfamiliar with the ways of the world, she had believed him to be immensely powerful, until a hail of bullets that shot out of the flame of a smokeless fire, destroyed her pathetic illusions. She could not understand who was to make the decisions now and trembled with anxiety when Malalaï set off for school with three other adolescents who lived in the area. Every day her daughter brought back news of what was happening in the world: "They burnt a truck full of books for the schools, on the Kandahar road! They slaughtered the teachers and set fire to all the schools in the Nuristan region," The widow always nodded, no longer knowing which era she was living in; in which strange state of seclusion. The sun, the moon, the wind, wild animals and men bustled about outside. The open air belonged to males and stones. As for the women, cloistered within their walls and their veils, they ended up losing all notion of time. And who were they to believe, the Imam, the terrorists or the government? Before she had been widowed, when Malalaï was just a child, wives and marriageable girls were not supposed to approach the windows, and in fact all the window-panes were painted white. They were not allowed to go out without a *mahram*, an old or young male relative. The whip flayed the skin of those who displayed their ankles or laughed in public.

When he returned to the other widows on the floor above, the Unconscious locked himself away with his reading book. Barely aware of the birds calling and his fellow creatures who had just escaped from a madrasa, he tried hard to imitate Malalaï's musical voice. Spelling out the syllables was a way of drinking from her lips, but it was still only drop by drop that he could taste the saliva of the row of words. Thanks to the young girl's efforts, he had been admitted to the public school shortly after the invalid's death. Those who do not know how to read are terrified by the simplest formalities. Ma'Rnina nonetheless agreed to the idea of getting rid of the kid, although she would have far preferred to send him to the Koranic school. Since the beginning of these endless wars, millions of widows were waiting for a firm hand to keep their boys at bay. And of course the Imam did not make light of the Five Pillars.

It is only in the evening, after having greeted a large number of people in the staircase, with the whole neighbourhood frightened by the threat of a suicide attack or a likely raid by the government police that he finally resolved to face the two women's acrimony. One Eyed Alam had not yet returned. The neighbour through the crack sang voicelessly with his *rabab* reduced to a board. *Neither bent nor covered in rancid butter, he whispered, I am nothing but a poor disciple, a candle in the wind, a handful of bees on the tongue of the wicked. I cross the thousands of worlds. Each of them is a pilgrimage. In the river of speech, I cross the thousands of centuries in silence....* The old Sikh had not made an appearance at the paralytic's funeral, but his white beard poked in through the crack. The distraught child heard him thunder then: "*Galaza! Galaza!* Do not thrash about like the testicles of a galloping goat!"

Since he had started working, One Eyed Alam collapsed on his mattress after the evening meal. His headstrong nature was to blame; he could not bear the slightest admonishment. Ma'Rnina served him grumbling, her lips clamped together. Over the passing weeks something in his features changed. His dead eye grew even hollower and his cheeks took on the colour of birch bark. Ignoring the existence of the women almost entirely, he no longer spoke to his brother. One evening, Ma'Rnina was intrigued to see his face free of dirt and dust; while he handed over her share of his salary she remained silent and shrugged her shoulders.

Nonetheless, Alam began to come home later and later, forcing the two widows to stay up to warm the food. He no longer collapsed on his bed like an animal struck by lightning. One working day, the Unconscious who had returned from school caught a glimpse of him on his moped. Another time, he saw him come out of a café with some other young men, he looked happy and was wearing new shoes. One Eyed Alam who never missed his ablutions and the recitation of the *chahada* every morning, seemed preoccupied by important business. Before leaving the bedroom, he counted and re-counted a few banknotes and filled a small notebook with signs. Pretending to be asleep as he was scared of being scolded, his brother spied on him from under his long eyelashes. What was he dealing in since he left the mine? And why was he no longer interested in the latest details of Malalaï's inexhaustible beauty that he alone had the power to share?

In love, in the young girl's kitchen he soon forgot the One Eyed's enigmatic anger. The rage that he shared with those like him, the older boys on their mopeds who spat at the shadows of the schoolgirls or at the laughing women who worked in government offices. In front of the public school, the same young men threw stones at the windows and fled at top speed shouting the name of God under the noses of the dozing policemen, stationed there in their jeep.

In the secrecy of the boy's section of the school, the Unconscious learnt to read and count in books the rosary tellers abhorred. The coloured pictures and the fantasy of the calligraphies were illuminated solely by a young girl's face. What he discovered every day, despite the teachers' harshness, was like the inside of Malalaï's gaze. He came and went, captivated by Malalaï, using all kinds of ploys to gain access to the classrooms, without even being able to imagine why turbulent hordes wanted to stop him entering on certain days.

Life brought its own answers to the passage of time with its terrors and distractions, its quickening and its moments of indolence. Everything continued more or less precariously. The relative chaos left certain zones untouched, interstices of tranquillity abandoned to the discretion of a shepherd on his hill, or to a *hookah* smoker in a bazaar alley. The deadly raids and targeted bomb attacks in the surrounding areas, in the mountains or near the Pakistani border, the bloody intriguing between the district police, drug barons and rebel leaders, did not prevent shopkeepers and craftsmen, mine workers, a mixed crowd of children and the unemployed, from maintaining their habits of bygone days. Expectantly, threatened on all sides, between God and men, people managed, mindful of the seasons and the festivals, never clearly taking a stand for or against Satan and the fire in the blazing infernos. A gregarious shopkeeper was very likely to be found covered in blood before his stall, his turban stuffed into his mouth. The battalions of special forces active in the tribal zones multiplied their dangerous acts of violence, certain that once they had concealed their blunders, the terrorists would respond with devastating operations. The hunt for the insurgents nonetheless respected the borders arms dealers and recruits for the rebellion regularly slipped through. It was as if the actors in this cataclysmic battle, evil djinns and storm demons who had come from Pakistan, Iran, Chechnya and

Europe or America, were struggling to outdo each other as they kept topping up the old Afghani cauldron.

Meanwhile, women continued to prepare aubergines cooked in fermented sheep's milk, spicy rice and leek raviolis. The children in the area forgot the war as they played at it; brandishing roughly tied together bits of wood in guise of Kalashnikovs.

The old musician on the other side of the crack knew a proverb *Love never cries as blood cries.* When Malalaï's mother began to scream madly, the neighbours hesitated before opening their doors. Maybe there were assassins at work in the staircase. The cries were so terrible that a long shudder of terror ran through the whole building. Only the mountain child hurried, as if carried off by a wind. The widow had torn off her veil and was busy raking her cheeks with all her nails. "They killed her!" She ululated. "They killed my daughter!" Ma'Rnina and others finally identified the site of the disaster and emerged at last, timidly from their homes. Malalaï had been taken to hospital, she and three of her fellow students. Several masked and helmeted individuals on mopeds had cornered them in front of the school entrance. Holding water pistols, they had raised the upper part of the chadris to spray the girls' faces. It was like a game. They were all laughing uproariously. The water pistols were filled with vitriol.

They never saw Malalaï again; her mother moved. The sun had gone down on the tree of the staircase that smelled of spices and eucalyptus, where a mixture of murmurs from transistors, secular songs and calls to prayers unendingly mingled in the irregular din of shoes, children's shouts, clinking dishes and the gurgle of drains. Sitting on one of the steps between the ground and the second floor, waiting for a faceless miracle, the child was no longer interested in the naïve pictures hidden in books. He no longer went to school in fact. Nobody around him cared. The good weather had returned, scorching, filled with fragrance and dust. The street almost melted in the sunshine. In the cool of the landings, he listened to the vast din of the town. The jolting of mule-drawn carts, the amplified call of the muezzins who echoed each other from one mosque to another like steersmen in the fog, the backfiring of trucks and motorcycles and all this commotion of barking, shouting and stamping feet. A suffocating cat, its ears pricked up, sometimes came to find shelter at Malalaï's door. Then its severe owl's eyes stared unflinchingly at him. Weeks had poured their weight of torpor over the memories. There was no clear song left, not a laugh. For the Unconscious, time had come to a standstill. Sometimes he even cried for his father, as he was unable to fathom his sorrow.

Having returned home with a shaven head after one of his mysterious disappearances, One Eyed Alam no longer even deigned to eat with his family. A white cotton *koufia* over his shoulders, his mind elsewhere, he gulped down his soup standing by the sink. One evening he developed a fever and began to sob for no reason. He spent two or three nights whimpering in his sleep, then one morning, watched by Ma'Rnina who followed his every movement nibbling on a corner of her veil, he gathered his belongings in a large cloth bag. "I'm joining the Jihad," he said. "We are going to put down the foreign enemy and the traitors!" His bag over his shoulder, he set a bundle of Afghanis down on the table. His hand already on the door handle, he looked at his young brother and his haggard mother with a long disheartened gaze, then he suddenly began to shout: "What do you think? That I'm going to live like you, like a beggar? You dare judge me? God is guiding me towards victory!"

Shortly after his departure, for the first time they clearly heard the Disciple singing behind his crack:

True, He was at the beginning
True, He was through the Ages
True he will always and forever be.

10

At the Northern tip of the Pantin cemetery lies an area that has no defined shape, nor certain existence. It is squeezed between the industrial area of les Vignes and the fan of train tracks stretching into the distance up to the sorting shed at Noisy-le Sec. More elusive than a meander through the infamous fringes of a nightmare, in the depths of its confusion it conceals one of those geometrically defined labyrinths located near avenue de la Déviation or Chemin Latéral, that one only escapes through forgetfulness. There is nothing to be seen, only concrete enclosures and iron hedges interrupted by wasteland, tunnels and bridges. Empty shells of factories from another age abound, along with glass and cement factories turned inwards upon their manufacturing secrets. Deserted roads reveal sudden vistas dominating the suburban plain of Saint Denis in Villemomble or Perreux. Between Romainville fort and the multitudinous citadels of high-rise structures and the rows of low buildings overlooking the surrounding suburb on the heights, a grey sun pierces the smog and mist through the clusters of blackberry and cotton bushes. Between two harsh train whistles, in the heartbeat of the coaches, the murky silence of these wastelands can be deciphered—rumble of aeroplanes taking off or landing, vibration of high tension lines, fluvial rustle of traffic blocking motorway access roads, insect hum of mopeds and other two wheelers on some avenue Barbusse or Vaillant-Couturier. Nothing really attracts the gaze here, in these hazy confines of emptiness that a startled flight of starlings momentarily translates into panic, opposite the unevenly backlit landscape of warehouses and fences. Boundary roads: strips of aimless, unending asphalt framed by two edges of beaten earth that run along worksites given over to vegetation, hauling companies, burnt out parking lots, factory buildings, most of which are abandoned. A street known as les Déportés, paved with old fashioned cobble stones dissolves into a wasteland. It seems to pull itself together as it passes a few structures, garages, warehouses, ancient factories. Then at the corner of the only inhabitable house, a sort of decrepit driveway runs along a bright hedge topped with barbed wire, a dead end alley that topples into a sudden drop into the suburban sky. An iron over bridge, inaccessible, fades into the hollow of a copse of thorns above a ruined staircase leading to former market gardens. Now they are invaded by rows of excavations, rapidly topped by narrow stucco monuments. A cemetery's new home, running lengthways, sheltered by a thicket of neglected cypress trees. Beyond, are occasional industrial buildings destined for demolition according to the boards nailed to the doors long ago; the horizon recedes in interminable metal and concrete designs, arrows, diamonds, towers, low rows. An icy impression of escheat hangs over this zone. Only misguided pedestrians venture here, taking it for a shortcut between the Ourcq canal, the ever haunted stations of Drancy and Bobigny and the immense field of the dead in Pantin, where the alleys are named after trees. Nowhere, even in the worst sections of the Courneuve or Clichy suburbs, does solitude assume such a murderous, inescapable shape.

The brick factory impasse nonetheless has no dearth of visitors, furtive pedestrians, powerful vehicles, emaciated night owls, mopeds from the neighbouring housing estates. The former brick factory stands in a square courtyard sheltered by high coal chimneys. Its halls are open to the winds, the numerous terraced warehouses are adorned with hoists and the annexes, made of glass and metal. The place inspires neither greed nor bravery. This is what both the inhabitants as well as the visitors like about it. The position of the ovens, set in a semi circle, defines a space with several entrances, under pools of light provided by the truncated or knocked down chimneys. This is where the Kosovar has his headquarters.

For the moment, half a dozen regulars are warming themselves around a brazier squeezed into an oven chamber. Young Samir is one of them, a hairless gorilla with sea tortoise eyes; he thunders on despite the elation brought on by smoking grass. His huge fists stuck into a sort of muffle made of two torn pockets of a leather jacket, he asks everyone to be reasonable. Mehmed, 1m 60cm tall, replies that his common sense stinks of cockroaches. "The Kosovar isn't an idiot, if not for the girl, he would have abandoned the Darkies and the Kaffirs ages ago!" Samir reveals all his missing teeth and jerks with laughter. "You make me pee! The Kosso he's a brother. He doesn't give a sh...t about the junkie..." Barely older than Samir, for once Yann does not get worked up. He spits on the ground, unconvincingly. Even taller than the gorilla, but as thin as a stork, he crosses his long West Indian handballer's legs in several places. "Don't worry, clown! We don't need a gun. She'll fold quickly, the Poppy, too ripped. She isn't worth anything now."

Other faces glimmer in the shadows where occasional embers glow. A few young people from the housing estate on the Heights or the one on the Plateau, sworn dealers who have come to take delivery and the only veteran in the band, old Roge. He strokes his yellowed tobacco chewer's beard, wondering what his immediate future might hold. He has nothing left but a foam mattress in a quiet corner of the factory. One morning they will find him frozen, like the kid huddled by a brazier, teeth chattering, between two trips to the Bobigny mall. Dependable, Roge keeps his eyes open and wets his throat on the Kosovar's tab. His sponsor has not been back since the area was last locked down by the drug squad and the anti-bandit service. The cops are after him for minor crimes, car theft, carrying a prohibited weapon, grievous bodily harm; they intend to put him away for a few years at least. For the moment, he's taking stock with the gypsies at Aulnay or hiding out in the housing estate on the Heights. The last time he had wanted to clean up the squat a bit, get rid of the tramps and the two old style dealers, twin brothers, arrived from Istanbul, who claimed to be working on their own. Someone had taken revenge by giving him up; nothing surprising there. Everyone here is scared of the Kosovar, even his acolytes. They seem to know that in another life, he used to kill without a second thought. It is written in his eyes. Nevertheless, he accepts parasites like himself, an old broken-down drunk, or the kid that appeared out of nowhere. To say nothing of this poor dopehead, more baked than a horde of beetles. Poppy must have gone to ground at the nanny's in the house, or up there in the runaways' makeshift tent. She has not left the dead end for months. Everything has gone wrong because of her. Roge keeps muttering: this girl is really bad luck. She's hard cheese. He has known since the Kosovar started making everyone take care of her, or at least watch out for her. But the first who gets too close is roughed up, chucked out, swept away. Apart from the kid. He even seems to accept him in this jungle, only to serve as a messenger between him and her in case there's a stink. The

Caïd's jealously seems to be the real thing. How would he know how to fuel an emotion? Nothing to do with love. After all, it's the Kosovar himself who is providing the young madam with slow death. The Turks just have to keep it together, so do the heavies from the housing estate on the Heights, who come for their supplies, and the ones from the Marches Sèches and the Plateau. Roge doesn't give a toss about this black market bizness, all these peddlers creeping about. He's only interested in saving his skin. Fifteen years in the army, as many in prison, and then the street to end, have only left him spahi instincts. Looking down the mouth of a bottle, he doesn't miss any of the sleazy sell-outs and other grassing this disparate band of dopers gets up to; sh...t heads or snow tasters. He, the Roge, sticks to gut rot. His head survives as it explodes in alcohol or dynamite. Corridas aren't for old horses. He laughs between gulps. What bothers him is why the Kosovar has dumped a kid on them. Squatting on his heels, the little black kid watches with a macaque's seriousness. The street kids who live off nothing and die of even less, he had often seen them in Africa or Asia, beggars, pickpockets, fresh meat, shoe shiners. There, it is understandable, the poor scatter their seed as widely as they can, like bushes in arid land. It is something new in this part of the world. For sure, les Vignes and its surroundings are dodgy and have nothing to do with civilisation. A rubble desert bordering industrial blockhouses and irrevocable refugee camps that have turned into housing estates. A place to play dead.

But there is an argument over by the braziers. Samir is waving a 7.35 and swears he will waste the squealers. Roge, tired of these insults, takes a long swallow; he notices how placid the child is as he remains crouching like the Fellahs. "Hungry? Do you want something to eat? What's your name then?" Alam has not stirred: he studies the old man on his pile of bricks, dirty, stinking in

his tatters, a balaclava raised over his bear's ears. Ten steps away
Mehmed shifts about, a nervous hand before the barrel of the gun.
"When the guys from down there get here, you can play at being
a killer!" Yann swings his arms rippling with muscles above the
men's heads. He points his index finger at each of them in turn.
"The Bedouins down there have their moles. They know exactly
what we're up to. There are some here who keep them informed."
The Roge grumbles, already drunk. He knows these little yobbos;
all mad, all squealers. Not one of them knows how to hold his
tongue. The first trashy writer can get what he wants out of them.
He will always find an idiot ready to bring out his artillery hidden
in the false ceilings in the common areas, so that he can pose for
the photo with his sub-machine gun, his cap concealing his young
face. Apart from the Kosovar, they're empty shells, just about good
enough to make decent corpses. The slackers even delegate the kid
to deliver sticks of hash at the mall. The handsome guy would not
be happy if he knew. He protects youth in his own twisted way.

The insistent sound of a horn scatters the gathering. At the
brick factory dead end, every visit could be a trap. In the cement
staircase, Alam skims his finger over the scar under the ear that
is missing a lobe. Just half a centimetre and the bullet would
have pushed through his temple. Nobody cares how long his hair
is. Apart from Mehmed who called him a girl. Others, like old
Roge, think he's a gypsy. When he had arrived at the factory a
few Sundays ago, the youngest in the gang had hurled nuts and
bolts at him. The older ones had laughed, hands stuck in their
pockets. "No gypsies here!" they murmured lazily. And then the
girl had appeared, staggering, her almost white hair in her eyes.
She looked every bit like a ghost, emaciated, with her transparent
skin, her mad gaze. "Leave him alone", she had shouted, hiccups
in her voice. "It's my brother who sent him". As he entered, Alam

had uttered Yuko's name. Everyone knew Poppy's brother had drowned in the Marne, trying to escape the security services at the detention centre for minors. And at the brick factory, nobody thwarted the Kosovar's protégé. He did not have any kind of acknowledged relationship with the junkie, he even kept her at a distance, tired of her demands. Her decline, something he could have considered himself largely responsible for, distressed him visibly. In return, Poppy accepted the suburban Caïd's pity that only provided her a pathetic squat above a cemetery. Before they had ended up in the danger zone of les Vignes, before this little gang war that ruined the atmosphere, the two of them must have shared almost happy times.

"Where have you been?" says the young woman, slipping out of one of the yourte-like structures, made of café awnings, salvaged from an area that was being demolished. "I've been waiting more than an hour for you". Alam extricates a large orange and bag of powder from his anorak. The generator set up in an open area hums continually. Light bulbs flicker above the shelters. "Quick, come inside the tent", exclaims the young girl, suddenly cheerful. Sitting cross-legged she has pulled her arm out of the turtle neck sweater and a pink patterned bodice, revealing the chafed areola of a breast under her delicate shoulder muscles. Within seconds she has prepared her dose, heated the spoon, pumped the liquid. Her skinny fingers seem to be undoing a spider's cocoon. As the needle penetrates the crook of her arm above the tourniquet, Poppy meets an antelope's gaze. She laughs loudly for a brief moment. "By the way, how old are you? Eleven, twelve?" The heroin courses through her veins, golden queen who occupies no realm. The deliverance is compensation for the waiting. An empty joy, nameless, titillates memory. Ecstasy replaces the filth of living. Poppy sighs and collapses, completely revealing her chest. In the radiant descent into the palaces of happiness, a miniscule part of her attention attaches itself to the boy's dark eyes. "You've never tried? I mean, injecting it..." Alam studies the junkie gravely, as her scrawny frame leans down from a balcony of paradise. Cannabis and alcohol, heroin fumes on an aluminium sheet, ether and even burnt glue, he had tasted them more than once, in Kabul as well as in Istanbul or in the sewers of the station in Rome. All the street kids did it more or less regularly, the thousands of refugees, those who had fled their villages, those who refused to join the insurgents. Their only ambition was to earn enough money and to leave, to strike a deal with a vaguely honest escort, to reach the other world, the one they saw in the pictures awash with joy. Those who grew addicted died where they were. He had not stayed there. He would not stay here either, at the brick factory dead-end.

"Will you go to England with me?" The sentence came to him ready-made, new in his mind. Was it the sight of Poppy's white breasts, the way her hair fell into the crook of her skinny arm, or the sad grimace on her lips when the needle poked into her vein? She has straightened slightly. Gold spangles spurt out from between her eyelashes. She smiles instead of answering. Her face seems to have fallen off a statue in a church. Her lips, now pale, pluck a petal of light. "Peel the orange for me", she says, inclining her palm till the fruit falls into Alam's lap.

11

They had not wanted him in the mines, nor in the foundries, even less in the wire or tin-plating works. He was far too young. For months, the Unconscious had been sleeping at the gates of the town, in the cockpit of a burnt out, dismantled Soviet tank, reduced to a skeleton. To earn even less than a dollar a day, he had to work from morning to nightfall. For a while he had joined the shoe shiners and the windscreen washers, despite the fights and the ferocious control exercised by the intermediaries, the ones who lent the shoe shine boxes. Very soon, young people in canvas trousers and expensive sneakers offered him work, delivering packets of opium resin under the police force's very nose. These middle-men who employed him on an occasional basis, offloaded on to him the greater part of the mission entrusted to them by one of the Caïds. They only handed over a miniscule fraction of what they earned to the little delivery boys. There were a lot of children ready to risk everything for a few Afghanis. As everywhere where the war economy encouraged the worst kind of dealing, the cowardly adults depended largely on this workforce that had nowhere to turn. The crowd of teenagers scurrying in all directions or hailing their regular customers lent the streets an air of false gaiety; this explosion of youth frantically trying to survive as their mummified ancestors looked on, was due only to the intangible vitality of a people.

On the fringes of the town, in the evenings, when the jackals were yapping in the hills, the Unconscious was well aware that others like him were lying in ambush everywhere, under the cover of dusk. Crevices and ruins, carcasses of vehicles, barns, were sometimes visited by the crowd of orphans and the night made these spaces even more attractive. His closest neighbour, about twelve years old, had covered over a bomb crater with metal sheets and boards. Along with the others of his kind, he tempted the devil every night, assured of making enough money to leave even faster this way: they had to lead the dealer's convoys through the plateaus, using short cuts that the rebels had riddled with mines. When a child blew up, others took his place. The Unconscious envied the peace of the stars on the horizon and the wolf's solitude as it howled at the moon. As soon as he nestled in the scrapped iron tank, a lost voice inhabited his dreams. Ma'Rnina had chased him off a long time ago. There was not enough money. Even death would not have been able to feed him. But the staircase held him prisoner. The dominos of the steps swung before him. Malalaï was calling for help. He could not move. The hall of the staircase was rotting like the inside of a skull. Strips of flesh steamed against the temporal bones. From within, a familiar voice faded into an echo. "Help me, help me!" it said. The whole building knew she had thrown herself out of a window, that Malalaï had jumped out of the window at the hospital. All that was left of her was a wandering voice that begged incessantly. A lost voice that would call out to him unendingly. Malalaï! The veil of darkness covers her forever.

Up at dawn, before the cocks and the goats, the Unconscious ran to wash himself at the caravan fountain. All the treasures of the earth and the sky joined forces at this hour. The suspended avalanche of rocks and the infinite plain bathed in light, glorified the shade of the roads. As day commenced, with the sun and the constellations in perfect alignment, a theatrical flow of gold and azure momentarily whisked the mind off on the falcon or skylark's wing. Then the great mirrors of dawn suddenly shook, transforming the streams of stars into a single forge's firebox, and the air filled with birds, into a dark, dead land. During this mysterious parenthesis, the world had afforded him a last hope of meeting again. The purple line of the hills stood out now from the night of the mountains. They formed a gigantic recess for the constellations, from where the insurrection seemed to be blossoming as bloody lava spurted out of the monstrous steel volcano continually incarnated by the coalition bomber planes. Caught between two fires, wracked by the Mullah's sharia and the collateral damage caused by the missiles, the decimated populations were abandoning their villages and their crops. Fleeing the hell of the battle-ragged hordes gathered around urban centres. The Unconscious had seen several refugee camps develop in this manner. Entire families of farmers besieged a market square or a burnt out school field, only to sink to the depths of misery. Swarms of children, more destitute than the hardened street hordes, paced the wastelands and the dumps looking for combustible materials, bits of plastic and other debris.

With their constant harassment, the guerrilla had infiltrated these outskirts so efficiently, that only the poorest dared move around without an escort. Unless they wanted to take up arms as they had no other choice. Appropriated by the rebels, the cemetery in the Southern zone was better defended than a small regular army fort. Every day a father or a child walked towards the fence, risking everything, ready to be shot down; their sole intention was to beg for help. The less fortunate, who had been forcibly enlisted, would not come back alive. Only burials took place peacefully, with the blessing of the over-armed bigots. The Unconscious never went near the tombs. He ran missions for twenty to thirty Afghanis. He and those like him would fall one day, when their turn came, their arm shot through or with a bullet to the head. In the meantime, he hugged a few more notes to his skin, next to his heart, as he ate his olive bread.

One evening, just like any other, as he was getting ready to settle in for the night at the controls of the tank, the surrounding mountains began to rumble. He first thought it was an earthquake. In Kandahar, earthquakes are usually accompanied by an unusual bellicosity. Almost immediately explosions rocked the outskirts of the town. While the air force pounded the insurgents' support bases, the latter massively attacked the government forces, sowing panic in the mafia organizations and amongst the mine managers. The battle was limited to the advanced posts on this side of the town however. A hail of fire forced some of the assailants back behind the rocks along the foothills. Covered by innumerable concealed shooters, others streamed towards the old cemetery that soon became the main target of the private militia who had rushed there to provide support. Tombstones flew under the heavy impact of mortar fire and missiles. This firework display seemed to push back the creeping dusk. His head poking out of his bomb crater, the young mine dancer rejoiced: many of the grenades falling all over the place did not actually explode. And that was another market. But a volley of fire finished him off ten metres from the tank. A scarlet jet sprayed the metal sheets. He screamed in pain and blown to pieces, tumbled, to the depths of his tomb. The Unconscious screamed too. He had crawled out of the cockpit and shouted up at the murderous sky. Back from their pounding, for form's sake the US Air Force hunters flew low over the burning hills. Still loaded with ammunition, the French support helicopters haphazardly sprayed the pockets of resistance. The Unconscious set off running aimlessly straight ahead, his arms in the air, as if overcome by the chaos. In this apocalyptic din, his voice was no louder than that of the ashy curlew or the gerbil on a quiet day. Blinded, tripping over stones or rocket shards, he ran through the hail of projectiles and the smoke, feeling as if he was walking over a river of sparks.

Other shouts rang out from within the cemetery and from the rocky strongholds in the distance: the leaders were calling to their men to fall back. In the confusion, incongruous troops weighed down with weapons retreated in a dispersed crowd. Unravelled turbans flew in the wind, in the purple streaked dusk. The child, who had just tripped over a headless body, remained lying on his stomach, suffocating, scanning the ground for the head, lost amidst the tombstones. A rebel dragged him up with one hand, a giant loaded with a bundle of weapons taken from victims from both sides. "Come on, walk!" he says. "We're getting out of this damned cemetery." Behind him, around him, everywhere, the stream of insurgents falling back drew him into the now opaque night.

As hollow as a sea after a storm, the silence dissolved little by little into tenuous sounds, short bird calls, the hiss of springs, the moans of the wounded transported on the backs of mules. As they progressed, the mountain exerted the blind force of its magnetism. A sort of fundamental peace washed over everyone's mind. Still deafened by this baptism by fire, the recruits stumbled behind the loose crowd of veterans. In several rows the rebels and their prisoners, young boys and adults, climbed the first foothills. "The journey will be long", says a horseman who had just dismounted, his chest packed with cartridge belts. The clink of weapons and the rhythmic click of feet guided each of them through the darkness of the gorges and the valleys. The mules brought up the rear, loaded with the dead and the heavy machine guns. On the slopes above the dwarf forests and poppy fields that were barely concealed by food crops, the silhouettes stood out gloomily under the wan light of the stars. Sometimes a ledge crumbling under a mule's faltering step echoed lingeringly in the escarpments. Very high up, above the footpaths, shone the perennial snow. An irregular shower of meteorites revealed the silhouette of the peaks. Here and there, torrents sparkled like molten iron. From the depths of the night rose the nurturing fragrance of poppy flowers.

The grey of the early hours soon unravelled the shifting mists and shadows. The insurgents walked on for a further part of the day still hidden by the sewers, beyond the Senjaray and Arghandab roads. They took care to avoid the groups of tribal people along the valleys who were paid by the government. They walked freely into the Gulbahar district almost entirely under Commander Muhib's control.

Reeling with exhaustion, the Unconscious recognised the sand coloured landscapes before him. The fatigue, along with his sudden snatches of memory stunned him with images torn from the intimate contours of recollection. They came in fragments or in flashes, fleeting, lightning effigies. Several times he had to rub his eyes in order not to fall flat on his back. Overwhelmed by sleep for a few seconds, he thought it was in a dream that he was returning to the area surrounding the village where he was born. He was dumbstruck when the slow moving troop crossed the place from one end to the other. No one came out, not an old lady, not even a cat. His village was reduced to rubble, pitted with bullet marks. Only the mosque was still standing.

In the distance, on a hillock planted with red poppies, about a dozen tombs were visible, marked by slight frames made of branches on which brightly coloured strips of rags wafted in the wind. After another halt to pray, the troop continued its retreat in a more relaxed manner. The enemy had lost any hold over these territories. They no longer had any guns or knives to turn against the troops, no one left to hate or to implore. Apart from the unlikely arrival of a squad of battle helicopters, the rocky outcrops were no longer to be feared. In addition, sentinels perched on knolls were already passing on the news of their return. Between two granite peaks, in a terraced valley above the steppe leading to the sterile heights of Pakistan, a company of armed men seemed to emerge from the mist. Lower down, in the flowering poppy fields, below the orchards and pastures where black-headed sheep roamed, a few farmers wearing embroidered tunics and turbans laboured peacefully amidst a large flight of wood pigeons. As they met, in a single voice the ritual victory cry rang through both columns. One laden with dusty weapons and shapeless bags, the other emerging even more euphoric with its mixture of features and garments announcing the presence of diverse groups amidst the Pashtuns. Pakistanis from the refugee camps in tribal areas, former Mujahedin, Uzbeks, Turkmen or Baluchis, dismissed by the warlords and other felons belonging to the defunct Northern Alliance.

At the height of the chaos, as weapons were brandished in the speckled light, a young, lean man, an assault rifle over his shoulder and a blue headband across his forehead, turned around laughing with a slow dancing movement, before crying out in surprise. He rushed over, his arms widespread, an expression of mad gaiety on his wounded face that looked even younger under its statutory beard. "You, here, Unconscious!" he kept shouting, thumping his brother in the ribs to welcome him. "So you finally found me!" Darkened by the sun, his shoulders had filled out, although a wolf's skinniness hardened his features; One Eyed Alam had lost his brazen city boy look. Even his voice that used to be musical, with feminine intonations, had gained in assurance and held a nuance of irony, as if nothing really surprised him, although his words expressed a certain confusion. "And the family?" he pretended to be interested, before adding as if aside, "bah, what little is left of it!" On these terraces that overlooked the beautiful tapestry of crops above the plain, amongst the mules and the horses, the canvas bags full of vegetables and the crates of weapons, the rebels were calling out to each other as if it were market day. Within a few minutes, One Eyed Alam had introduced the new recruit to about twenty taciturn bearded men who nodded, wishing him indifferently either victory or martyrdom. Everyone came and went, moving between caves furnished with pickings from the devastated villages, tents taken from caravans and worksite sheds buried under camouflage nets in the shadow of a pine forest. Sparingly posted on the hills, the sentinels dressed as shepherds were more concerned with the excitement provoked by the arrival of their comrades than the hostile surroundings. The state of alert was so normal that one could believe it forgotten. Thus the mosquito buzz of a reconnaissance plane circling above the mountains did not even cause the Commander's bodyguards to raise their eyes, as he came out of the woods where he had been examining the heavy artillery recovered from the enemy. As he passed him, Ustad Muhib pretended to glorify his young lieutenant's valour. "And this is your brother, this fellow? May God bless him: he will make a good soldier". To express his agreement, One Eyed Alam thumped the child affectionately. "I'll teach him myself how to handle the weapons". The Commander guffawed winking at his guards. "He'll learn with the other kids. We have our instructors! But I'm counting on you to set an example..." One Eyed Alam's salute to his leader was marked by apprehensive respect. Then he made an awkward gesture intended for his brother who was asleep on his feet. As if to say: "That's what you think!" Without further ado he took his hand and led him away towards the fields. A muezzin perched on a basalt dome struck up the call to prayer. Instantly the ant like agitation ceased: in silence they all turned towards Mecca. The farmers at the bottom of the slopes imitated the rebels. Carried along as if in a dream that was even set against the same backdrop as his former life, the Unconscious could only recognise his elder brother. None of the poppy cultivators belonged to his village. "Where have they all gone?" he asked when the fighters stood up. One Eyed Alam began to snigger. "You didn't see the graves? Blunders made by the coalition and the government forces! The survivors have run away to Kandahar or crossed the border. Those who stayed behind regardless were hanged or decapitated as traitors, even the women, even the children. The farmers you see in our poppy fields are Pashtuns who have come from Pakistan, farm workers, poor sharecroppers. They settled here with the Commander's blessings. There's nothing to understand!"

12

The youngest of his age group, the Unconscious did not see any more of his brother as his trainers monopolised him. There was a thirty year old veteran, who had not hesitated to shoot a very young Tajik as an example. In his innocence the child had only used Commander Massud as a reference, seeing him as being as legendary as Alexander the Great or Aladin. The other was a belligerent mullah trained in the Pakistani refugee camps. The new recruits were learning how to take apart an assault rifle and reassemble it in seconds while paying attention to the school teacher's fanciful propaganda. Between sunrise and sunset, in addition to the five ritual prayers, not a day went by without forced marches, simulated fights with knives, volleys of plaster grenades, simulated suicide attacks. The difference with real war, his section leader explained, was the question of timetables. When it comes to killing or being killed, day and night cease to exist, as do schedules. At the provincial madrasa, for hours on end, the mullah forced the shaved heads to recite the points of doctrine dealing with the new Sharia. "You will be the last angels of a healing government!" he declared at the end of a martial oration. The man was renowned for his unorthodox enthusiasm: the officers had no qualms about correcting him before his audience. "It's the best hadith, the most authentic", he declared learnedly one morning to the visitors who had come to sit amongst the children. The Unconscious was not surprised to learn the mullah had been placed in quarantine. He had clearly lost his mind. Before sending him back to civil life, they imprisoned him for a few days in a shed, with a man who was a Kafir, a Bengali journalist whose exchange value was still being debated. This miscreant who had been kidnapped three months earlier during a raid, did not seem to be all there either.

The Unconscious did not have the heart to judge his teachers. Like the other recruited children, he was ordered to obey his instructors to the letter. In addition, obeying orders was a sort of consolation for the youngest. The first time he had to use a weapon was near a small town occupied by contingents of the national army. They were to neutralise a checkpoint so they could capture one of the armoured vehicles, fill it with explosives and use it to blow up the garrison; all that in record time so as not to leave the enemy time to react. The attack on the checkpost was like a training exercise. Supported by experienced rebels, three children, including the Unconscious, aimlessly fired hails of bullets at the adversary while other insurgents attacked the target from the rear, sheltering behind a crumbling embankment. Stones fell against the vehicles. Almost simultaneously, two soldiers collapsed. The others tried to escape the cross-fire. One of the young recruits fell in turn, right in the middle of the road. The Unconscious did not react, but he bit his lips. The order in battle was not to save one's comrades, but on the contrary, to fight even harder. His rifle wedged under his arm, he walked directly towards the target. Insults and shouts rang out behind the chevaux de frise. Then there was silence. The rebels who had just taken over the checkpoint began by shooting the wounded with a bullet to the head. One of the still able soldiers begged, his hands folded. The death blow pushed his face sideways. Meanwhile other insurgents filled a jeep with jerry cans full of petrol and explosives. But a rocket shot from an army half track that had come to their aid ruined the commando's mission. The Jeep caught fire and the assailants dispersed amongst the rocks, starting with the two who had been designated as martyrs. Warned by the shouts, the Unconscious did not stop shooting through the flames. He had not been taught to run away from fire. When the jeep exploded, thrown to the ground by the blast, he saw pieces of metal fly past above his head. Back at the camp he sank into a deep torpor, with a few burns, an open wound on his skull and the congratulations of the hierarchy to show for his adventure. The boy of his age wounded in the stomach, lay on the road calling all night for his mother, while a stone carver from Kandahar placed compresses on his face. At dawn, the morning prayer rose to cover his moans.

By day or night, in the deepest countryside or on the fringes of urban areas, there were many more operations, all more or less dangerous. Each expedition ended in blood and terror. Surprised at still having a head on his shoulders, the Unconscious pondered on the false miracle of these battles. Anyone who boasted about them had to have survived yet again. Why had the comrade who set out on an equal footing and so valiantly, lost his legs and why was he biting on his shroud crying blood from his guts? Why did he himself have the power to sacrifice or spare beings made up of a few dozen years of existence on this earth and who were filled with a mass of memories, secrets, aspirations? They encouraged him to throw bombs at faces and scream for joy for reasons of sanctity or honour. One full moon night, accompanied by a young Pashtun commando brought back from Pakistan, he had burnt down the new school of a village that had fallen back into government hands. The children who studied there looked on in terror. "What right do you have to destroy my school?" the teacher, who had emerged from his dwelling in pyjamas, had exclaimed. He had not had the time to protest. "Shoot the unfaithful", the leader of the group had ordered.

The Unconscious went on long nocturnal walks along rutted roads filled with potholes, or along perilous ridges, loaded with grenades and cartridge belts, and sometimes with a mortar cannon over his shoulder. He was fed a thick mess of mutton, broad beans and dairy products. The confusion of daily violence with its sudden outbursts and the echo of hysterical orders, mysteriously followed on from prayer times when the most belligerent suddenly asked the heavens to show them mercy. Life was only a smokescreen, a brutal illusion that you cut across with a simple gesture. They slit people's throats and massacred without hatred, as if they were killing the Aid el Kebir sheep, as a sacrifice and in accordance with the law. God was responsible for replacing the son of men who died in war with rams and goats, lying on the left side at the gates to paradise, in the glory of the beyond. At least this is what the Unconscious imagined when an adversary, so similar to his companions in the struggle, was thrown to the ground and wounded. While he lacked the usual ferocity to be found in ill-treated children, an inflexible rage took hold of him when his section leader allowed him full rein. With his shouting and persecution the latter treated him more harshly than an enemy, whose only concern was to finish him off. Was the aim of all this mad exasperation and this cruel abuse just to forget the body, to attain silence and prayer before the crushing emptiness of the mountains? A man at war was only a machine to bend to one's will. The Unconscious obeyed, his gaze steady, deprived of fear and resentment. Something within him was destroyed, extinguished, cold, like these corpses of wild boar, killed only for amusement and left to the vultures.

Some evenings after the ritual weapon cleaning sessions, he lay down under a donkey's head, trusting the hoofs and believing he was resting peacefully, open eyed on the vast hidden snow of a sky full of stars. The rebels crouching here and there around the peat embers contained by bits of tiles, drank unending cups of sweet boiling tea. Others, whose job was to polish the pieces of artillery, smoked shapeless butts or slim earthen pipes. Under the long ears framing a quadrant of the zodiac, everything took on an indulgent air. "Who are you? What is your name?" asked a distant voice. Sleep was inhabited by shadowless images. An old cleric, suffering from hepatic pains recited the ninety-nine names of God to express his suffering.

Free for once after he had been relieved of his duty guarding the prisoners, One Eyed Alam told him boldly of his plans for the future. It was simple, he was fighting the foreigners with his Pashtun brothers, and with his good eye he supervised the poppy crops. After all, one of the fields swept by the desert wind belonged to them and the others had been confiscated from the villagers, uncles and cousins. When the time came, he would circumvent the share croppers and the Pakistani day labourers who paid rent to the insurgent leaders in the district. He had already introduced himself to them as the person in charge, the one who knew the Caïds, all the dealers from Kandahar. Alam cut a fine figure, his patch over his eye, a revolver in his belt. "Do you remember our father?" he said. "A hobo, just like millions of others in this damned country. He had no choice but to grow them, these flowers! Farmers have no other way of keeping their families alive. *Opium Poppy!* May the whole world die of them. We could even do without the dealers. Instead of selling them the resin, we should make the morphine here; it's

not that difficult with a bit of equipment. I saw how they did it
in town. Then we would do without the Khan, the money would
go to the producers, we would supply the whole world! There's
no lack of labour here either. Look, the Pakistanis down there,
they work for whoever pays best, those who protect them, mullahs,
owners, or warlords. In a few years, believe me, if the foreigners
don't send in their machine guns we'll all be rich..." Leaning against
a tree, One Eyed Alam began to laugh like a trilling blackbird.
Only the groaning of a wounded man under the infirmary tent,
reminded them of the gravity of the moment. But the weather was
good, nature filled the air with fragrance, and there had to be a life
after the war. The Unconscious liked listening to his brother hold
forth. Nobody was as glamorous as him in his eyes; he represented
everything he was familiar with, things, memories, the accent from
before. His brashness and pretentiousness did not matter. When
he deigned to approach him, the Unconscious retrieved a precious
memory from a time before the orders and threats, the poisoning
with words, the unmistakeable sound of weapons being reloaded.
He would long remember his slanting look, not really worried but
suddenly intense, on a day when there was a toss up to choose
two of the youngest, who in the absence of any women, would
be designated to play the martyrs. They had to blow up the police
station of a small town close to the desert. A commando operation
could have worked but with no hope of escape. The target was
exposed on all sides. A donkey weighed down with a bomb, led by
one or two kids was better than an armed group. One Eyed Alam
had not trembled, but a very faint expression of irony flitted over
his features the moment the star of death swiftly spared his brother.
The latter was in fact ready to sacrifice himself. When bullets
replace words, the survival instinct wanes along with hope. The
continual sight of suffering bodies, amputees, people executed to

make an example of them, soon turns into a farce. He had seen his companions burn rag dolls, scarecrows and kites just as seriously as they mowed down the enemy.

Nothing escapes violence; the world no longer exists. One slits the throat of a goat or a child with exactly the same movement. The moment a woman laughs too loudly or dances with another, they tie her up and kill her with sharp stones. Every man is betrayed by his shadow. A hallucination guides sleepwalkers whose hands are bloodied from tearing out another's heart. This is what the Bengali prisoner sometimes told his guards. By a stroke of bad luck, one night he was on duty, the Unconscious found himself with his elder brother at the door to the shed, under the immense expanse of a cave overlooking the poppy fields. Still amazed at people and what drove them, One Eyed Alam could not prevent himself from talking to the most garrulous or urging the taciturn to reveal their deepest secrets. A mixture of candid enthusiasm, good-natured indolence and unimaginable savagery in his moments of rage, made him more unpredictable than a stranger met the evening before. Although he feared him almost as much as the section leaders and the discipline-crazy instructors, the Unconscious could not help loving him.

That night, the hostage was highly amused at seeing a boy with antelope eyes and a tall one-eyed adolescent guard his door, their Kalashnikovs in the crook of their elbows. He asked the younger one if he liked war and, pointing to a nightingale in mid-song somewhere in the shadow of the branches, whether we should attribute the same value to human life as to this song in the moonlight. His fingers clenched around the bamboo poles of his prison, the hostage spoke of the charm of a time without servitude. One-Eyed Alam who was listening open-mouthed, expressed mocking confusion. What charm was he talking about? Had there even been a time before the war? "Those who inhabit this planet should change their ways", the Bengali replied calmly. "All God's creatures are made for love, the humans and the sheep, the fish in the sea, the jackals and the nightingales. Happiness belongs to he who refrains from wounding anything living, even a butterfly. This is the only worthwhile prayer. He who abstains from killing even a fly, knows no fear. He provokes no distress in other creatures. Those who commit endless acts of atrocity are not really guilty as ignorance is the first kind of violence..." Greatly amused, Alam brandished his automatic pistol at the hostage's throat: "And if I were to kill you like a dog, will it change the world in the slightest?" The prisoner nodded his head good-naturedly. "Certainly," he said. "In your young colleague's eyes, for example!" One Eyed Alam lowered the barrel of his weapon, giggling. "My colleague?" he said. "Ah! This devil of a younger brother! At the age of eleven he is worse than Commander Muhib himself!"

They had forgotten to relieve the guards at the fifth hour, as is the practice. Such a worthless prisoner, *à fortiori,* a pacifist to the tips of his fingers, could almost be forgotten despite the endless admonitions he addressed to the meat eaters. Emerging from a fuzzy dream of harmony, his eyes opened onto daybreak; the Unconscious shivered as his chin brushed against the cold barrel of his Kalashnikov. He immediately felt a dull threat. His eyelids blinked against the dancing light of the foliage. In the distance he noticed the poppy capsules, partially divested of their petals, bobbing in the wind like crowned birds' heads. Under his nose, the cane door hung open in the half-light. Passerines squabbled almost at his feet. So tiny, with their beaks like grains of wheat, they invested all their energy in these battles over a twig. The alarm was only raised after the first prayer. Standing up, trying to make sense of the scattered shouts, the young duty insurgent rubbed his eyes, blinded by the blaze of the rising sun. After issuing a series of orders, an officer with an eagle's profile, a ragged turban perched like a wing on his head, slammed his fist into his shoulder. The child almost crumpled, his breath knocked out of him, and he made an effort to stand at attention. No, he did not know how the hostage had escaped, he had not seen anything, he had fallen asleep. "You should be made an example of!" screamed the section officer, who pretended to cock an old Soviet, Nagant type revolver. Just then, alerted by the noise, Ustad Muhib arrived on the scene, relaxed. Close behind him a lieutenant, tensely clutching his sub-machine gun, seemed to crystallise all the tension of the situation. A smile on his lips, the commander placed a hand on the child's head. "What's going on now?" he asked calmly. The man with the predator's profile turned to point to the empty shed, the valley illuminated by sunshine and the petrified child. But nothing happened. Muhib asked each of them to get on with their regular duty. The day was spent in preparations: the upcoming raids and sabotages were to target the small towns in the Sangin area. A number of these villages had been taken back by the government troops after a sustained campaign by the coalition forces, supported by drones and strategic bomber planes. Crates of Russian weapons that had arrived on camel back from the Registan desert were opened feverishly. They exhibited the models in the sunshine, they shot volleys into the air or against the rocks, cheering loudly.

Daylight was waning. The farmers at the bottom of the hills had withdrawn to their makeshift shelters. As they progressed towards the heights, raising more dust than the hoofs of a caravan, a group of rebels held forth, gesturing. It was soon clear they were pushing an individual harnessed to a thick hemp rope ahead of them. Commander Muhib's face lost its cheerful expression. When the new arrivals reached the place triumphantly, he told them to be quiet and demanded they untie the young man. A circle immediately formed around One Eyed Alam. His distraught brother who had remained in the background did not understand what they wanted of him. Both of them had always obeyed the most enigmatic orders. He studied his older brother's cheeky expression with sudden terror. Why was he provoking the insurgent leaders with his lone eye? Ustad Muhib was standing apart from the group, his back slightly bent, legs apart. "Pray" he said with a strange gentleness in his voice. Alam did not grow pale; he raised his head in a defiant movement that served to hide his astonishment. "Go ahead!" he shouted. "Kill me if you want!" The commander slowly turned towards the silent group of fighters; he seemed to study them one after the other, scruffy bearded men, skinny adolescents that looked like goatherds, mountain men fiercer than bears, plump clerics in their waistcoats, gloomy looking children. "You, the Unconscious, come over here!" he finally exclaimed. Alam's brother advanced as he was ordered, fighting back his terror. "You're going to prove your loyalty to God and to our cause" continued Muhib. "We're all brothers here, except the traitors! You will kill him immediately! Move away from the One Eyed!" A wave of panic pushed back the rebels. Freed of his bonds, the young man cast a look behind him, towards the rocky slopes and the blazing horizon, as if to evaluate his chances of escape. "Wait! Wait!" he said, suddenly enthusiastic. "I have a gift for my little brother." From his pocket he drew out a stone heart, a beautiful emerald in its veinstone. "It's for you, kid. I found it in the copper mine, go on take it, it's all they left me!" The emerald rolled to a stop at the young boy's feet, he looked questioningly at the faces around him. Ustad Muhib expressed his impatience with a shrug. "Now finish off this wretched boy! Empty your clip into him!" Clutching his automatic pistol, the Unconscious clenched his jaws, horrified at feeling tears rise up within him. "Shoot, get on with it!" shouted his brother who had just torn the blue headband off his forehead. "Go on shoot! Let's get it over! You don't want to? Shoot, go on! I'm no friend of yours... You didn't know? I'm the one who shot acid at Malalaï!"

The spray of bullets cut One Eyed Alam in two. A layer of black blood spread in the dust. Satisfied, Commander Muhib crouched to pick up one of the casings. He offered it to the child, who had just been divested of his still smoking weapon. "Take this too," he said. "In memory of your loyalty".

13

Concealed behind the visor of his full-face crash helmet, the Kosovar crosses the Vignes industrial area crouching low over his handlebars. The area is no longer safe for him since the neighbouring gangs have got involved in arms trafficking. As he parks his motorcycle in a lock-up garage in the dead end, near an old van with somewhat deflated tyres, he remembers having spent more than one night in the back of it, before moving into the factory. He rapidly slips the pistol hidden under the seat into his belt.

Shades of purple, brought on by the April dusk, colour the faded corners of the buildings, the partially detached gutters and the zinc roofs. Since the assault launched by the canal gang a few days ago, the brick factory has been emptied of its occasional visitors. The losers have packed their bags and moved on to a more peaceful squat. The dealers have gone, so have all the others, the ones who no longer slept the peaceful sleep of the bourgeois, the accordion players, the men selling pewter Eiffel towers, a whole den full of highly useful extras who served to distract attention. Vast swathes of soot on the cement exteriors are a reminder of the Molotov cocktail attack. A few shotgun impacts show up, and far more serious, the rust on the big gate that was destroyed by anti-armoured plating weapons is clearly visible. The Kosovar is on his guard as he slips into the small paved courtyard. They are out to get him, he knows it, and killers do not always coordinate. Those in the know would like to get hold of the goods before they shoot him. The pit bulls from the canal have him in their sights now with the quiet approval of the small time local mafia, hot heads, gypsies and dealers. And they all have the blessings of the drug squad. This time his pride will not let him go to ground in the housing estate on the Heights, where he no longer has many friends. He will last out the siege with the few who are still loyal, at least until he decides what to do. During the Kosovo war in the North of the country he had found himself in far worse situations, confronted with the enemies' hydra like heads, secret services, militia, nationalists who had switched sides and local criminals. To say nothing of the American bomber planes that razed the family home along with the stew and the younger brothers. Barely older than Alam at the time, all he had known of the world was fear, disdain and violence. There, even the fresh warmth of love was a reminder of the chaos of the massacres.

His footsteps echo in the brick factory's deserted halls. "It's me!", he shouts as a password. Yann and Samir jump down from a metal walkway that leads to the foxholes on the floor above. The West Indian, who quickly regains his balance, points to the shattered windows on the canal side: "What are we waiting for to get going! I'll change the battery in the van!" Samir can only agree, his hands hanging at his sides. 'They'll be back in force, the bastards. They know we have some good stuff...' Unobliging, the Kosovar grabs the gorilla by the collar. "Forget it! We have everything we need here, right? And the people from the Heights will support us..." A blackbird's trilling deepens the silence. Yann nervously strikes a match. The flame between his palms carves out the contours of a boar's head. No one, in fact, is expecting anything more from the Heights or from the Marches Sèches and even less from the Plateau. The alliances have broken down since the Caïds' gamble to take over the intermediary dope market. A mere epiphenomenon, the trafficking of heavy weapons and explosives imported from the Balkans, is part of these new strategies: you just have to make the best of things! Everyone is looking out for himself leaving events to follow their course, the dealers, the mobs and the extremists—to wangle a gram of coke, hold up a post office or blow up the monument to the dead.

Standing on an outdoor platform on the first floor of the factory the Kosovar looks out over the sparse ocean of suburban lights. Constellations crossed by the fire dragon of motorways and the slow rockets of the trains, beneath the stormy palpitations of jumbo jets rising from Roissy airport. Night spreads over a dark world. There's nothing really preventing him from catching a flight to Montreal or Rio de Janeiro, only the sort of void digging into him, like a blade, just below his heart. He no longer expects anything from anyone else, from their fickle warmth. If not for Poppy and the kid, this world would be worth nothing more than a gaping hole in dead meat. "Where have they got to?" he whispers to himself. Lying on the floor, drunk, the Roge murmurs a vague answer. He raises himself a bit and cracks open a marble eyelid. "Where do you expect them to be? At the nanny's, in the house!" The old man is frightened at being associated yet again with the shipwreck of people he barely knows. When the canal pirates dock it will not make the general collapse any worse. A strange mystery hangs over the brick factory: just yesterday people came to negotiate a sale, there were good lookers in search of a stick of dynamite or a Kalashnikov, all that in the midst of bedlam. But at the first signs of danger, not a mouse in sight. Even the local vermin have abandoned the place.

The circle of light from a torch dances through the gathered shadows. Mehmed takes a look around the warehouses and alcoves under the high steel beams before joining his accomplices. "It seems quiet enough", he says. "We should look for another hideout though". The Kosovar does not reply. He greets the group and moves off. The crates full of weapons and explosives are readily available. There is nothing to prevent them staying where they are.

When he gives his name at the door of the house, he is struck by a feeling of déjà vu. A torn woollen shawl around her shoulders, the old woman opens the door indifferently. In her kitchen, she handles museum objects: the enamelled metal coffee pot, the flower patterned cups, the biscuit tin decorated with a landscape. "They're together all the time", she says. "They stare at each other for hours without moving. Sometimes they scare me." The Kosovar smiles involuntarily. From his jacket he draws out two black plastic packets, taped and tied, he sets them down on the Formica table. "Hide them for me as usual". The old lady agrees. She disappears for a few seconds and returns holding a letter. "It came yesterday, it must be for you". He tears the ends and pulls out different identification documents that he stuffs into his pocket without a word. Watching the door handle, he nods briefly. "Okay, nanny! Tell the kid I'm going to need him..." With these words, the Kosovar rises hesitantly and finally leaves the place, with the vague sensation that he has lost a miniscule chance of salvation.

Behind the door, Alam the Unconscious heard the Caïd's voice. He guesses his plans. Actually the man does not hide anything from him. Despite his generally ferocious nature, he behaves like an insecure father. With consideration and even a certain delicacy. As if in him, he had recognised an inviolable space.

In the back bedroom, lying on a pile of mattresses, Poppy trembles with a cold that is devouring her from within. Snow does not melt in blood. Her arm, pricked a thousand times by the delicious abyss and her brain full of lightning and night cause her terrible suffering. The piercings and tattoos that protect her from the naked ghosts of concupiscence create a pathetic armour of signs around her. Rocked by earthquakes, the dark earth of the past spits out its corpses. She remembers a childhood in the hands of patient murderers. Life is the product of a long, such a long infanticide. Who could she complain to though? There is no court for trampled memories. Fortunately Alam has returned to her side. He gets undressed, and watches her. His impala eyes see right into her depths, there where the flesh forgets itself. Alam is like an impala, the little African antelope, if man touches him, terrified by this mark of a predator against his skin, he will flee to escape himself, just as other impalas would have fled. He will run as far as he can without ever being able to stop. Poppy cannot help him; her legs can no longer run. Death lies heavily inside her. But as a wraith, every five or six hours, she remembers the kid sitting near her, and calls out to him from a great distance, with a voice so feeble he cannot hear it. Alam, my child, are you there? Solitude and love are the same embrace. Alam I am almost twenty and you, barely twelve, but you are a century older than I. Come closer, right up against this brazier of needles. Your too smooth skin is a mirror. Your face is the face of my child. Sleep on my breast, close your eyes; you have nothing more to fear. I will no longer tear myself away from the night's brambles. My strength will return. The wounds on my arms will heal like evening violets.

I will not vomit any more. Life will be born again in my veins. We will leave, you and I, for America. First, help me little brother, I need to switch this body on again. The syringe is in the sewing box, with the spoon and everything else. Help me quickly or I will die... Alam ties a blue ribbon around her arm; the flame of the lighter spits under the melted sugar. As she shoots up, lips trembling, Poppy encounters a gaze so sad that she giggles. "We call that feeding the monkey", she says with a sigh. The syringe falls out and rolls on the ground. One arm uncovered, her breasts exposed, the young girl sways. Her shirts slips off the other shoulder revealing an immense tattoo that runs all the way down to her hips. To the Unconscious, it looks like a shadow lying on top of her, its chest narrow, its hair undone. He tries to catch it in his hand. Poppy lets him do what he wants. "It's my twin sister, my little Siamese who died of fear", she says falling backwards. "I wanted to keep her close to me, as close as possible." Bending over her, the Unconscious contemplates the mad contours of her skin. Under her armpits, in the crease of the groin, along her thighs, lie mysterious vistas. From the navel where a gold ring gleams, up to the anemone palpitations of her violently blue eyes, runs the same dream fabric, the same rimless gaze, just like the infinite horizon of a landscape. Which of the two children fell asleep? A drop of blood forms, darker than a pupil. Just along the veins, the skin is exactly the colour of poppy flowers. A burst of stars pierces the skin of the sky. A freezing wind annoys the teats. But she is dizzy. Someone is dying; they can make out his dull moan. Is a poisoned mouse dying in a corner? All the suns burst out in hiccups. The pain slowly turns into an intense sweetness. Lips part on to very ancient words. "You who are and who will be..." Alam touches her cheeks, her eyelids. It is raining inside the house. The water runs down between her breasts, along her stomach, onto the twin sister's hips. Poppy's breathing grows faster; she pushes back the embrace of the huge tattoo. She looks like the ink figure inscribed on her skin. Their hair mingles. "Don't leave me", she murmurs again, her hands outstretched. "Never leave me". A train whistles in the distance. In the deserted immensity, she whimpers very softly. *It would be as easy for me to leave you as to leave my soul.* Time sags with all the midnight poppies. A dead woman's beauty glimmers in her mourning eyes. "Come", she says. "Sleep close against me". Alam travels through unknown skies. He crosses countries stiff with ice, countryside with sticky dresses and towns that raise their guard dog heads. They are chased off, he and those like him, they say: "The war is over, you must go home!" *Here I die every day; there I will be assassinated.*

Alam the Unconscious trembles against the feverish wound of a woman. They hear the rumble of motors. The glare of the headlights spreads like a fan over the walls and the ceiling. But he curls deeper into his night. His eyelashes create a lattice-work of shade. Poppy has raised herself onto her elbows, so pale in the rain of her hair. The oval slit of her eyes the colour of a gash, rests on the young boy's neck and chest. "I had already noticed the ear", she says placing her index finger on the bullet shaped scar just below the heart. Alam allows his face to crumple like a mist of heat. Sleep draws him from one labyrinth to another. In the oasis region where the Hundred and Twenty Day wind blows, in the biting nights of the Hindu Kush mountains, following snow leopard and wolf tracks, through the steppes and the marshes he walks, walks with a stone on his back. Wet cloth, sheets of blood sometimes hamper him. He walks between the flowering tombs of the fields. They hear sounds like the shots fired at a celebration. He is followed by children in rags, thousands of them from Kabul, as well as others from the sewers in Rome and the Ourcq canal..

But he wakes up alone in the room full of reflections. Poppy is breathing. She is also walking in the town, far from the street lights. The downpour soaks her to the skin but she feels fine. It looks as if the light falls in drops in certain places. Large water flowers, live jellyfish shine in the air. The street looks deserted; one can make out the contours of a church, trees shivering in all this dusk. Poppy is asleep her eyes wide open; she is sleeping the false sleep of the condemned and of martyrs. "How did it happen?" she asks, a hand pressed against his chest. As she receives no answer, she leans over a bit further and embraces him. "Who did that to you?" she insists. How would he know? You come out of a burning house, hands blackened, and you don't understand. How can he know what there was before death? Poppy wraps herself in the sheet and adopts the cruel attitude of little girls. She suddenly seems invincible, inaccessible, like the snow on the peaks. "They killed me too. They kill children with all kinds of objects". Her hands together, she begins to laugh like a statue, with a secret, cavernous laugh. But her eyes shine with a single diamond. This tear is the drop of water missing from the sea. Alam does not want to listen to her any more. A dizziness carries off the images. Draped in stone he calls out for Alam from the depths of his nightmare. His brother wants to speak to him from beyond separation and exile. His brother looks exactly like him. But he is a demon, a sort of angel with a murderous smile. His burnt hands come apart in strips. Was it he who released the hostage? Alam would like to save Alam. His words draw a flash of lighting and fall to the ground clinking like Kalashnikov casings. Which one of them has been rubbed out? Which one is dead, which one survived? Time conducts a war that is too slow and too cruel.

14

Three columns converged on the Sangin region, below the Gulbahar foothills. The Unconscious walked in Commander Muhib's footsteps. For weeks he has remained beside him, under his exclusive protection. With a guffaw, the war leader had promoted him to the position of aide de camp. In exchange, at every opportunity the child had to prove his endurance and his courage. His load was that of an adult soldier, with the rocket launcher as well sometimes. He was now included in all the forays. Ustad Muhib could not do without his mascot. In addition to the handsome girlish face, what appealed to him was the boy's disdain for intimidation manoeuvres in extreme situations and this cat like indolence amidst jackals and biting dogs. The kid would make an excellent suicide bomber one day. The commander did not like this idea though. One had to attain perfection before sacrifice. And then, the young soldier's company cheered his days as an uncompromising leader; at last, with him he could enjoy a few moments of tranquillity between tea and prayer time. For the moment, his automatic weapon over his shoulder, the Unconscious walked twenty paces away, a graceful genie between two limping giants. Since the middle of the night he had been climbing steep inclines and hurtling down ravines without a murmur of complaint. Silently, he advanced behind the column, ready for the worst. No one could have imagined and Muhib less than anyone, the stupor that inhabited his every moment. In the bivouacs, his head resting on his knees, he clutched an uncut emerald crystal and a copper casing in his fingers at the bottom of his pockets. A child's memory burns even in forgetfulness. He felt no fear. But he was beheaded in his dreams. Smiling strangers tore out his eyes; His blood splashed the faces of his mad mother and Ma'Rnina. There was no longer anywhere he could hide. Grenades hanging from his belt, he walked behind men overloaded with ammunition, ropes and canons. Great swathes of stars shone between the shadow peaks. The hooting of owls and the cry of jackals guided him more surely than the heavy insurgents' footsteps.

When the moon paled under the low branches, with a kind of sorrowful jubilation the Unconscious felt the dew running over his face.

Perfectly unperturbed, like a man out for a relaxing stroll, Commander Muhib led his troops to sacrifice. For him war was a condition common to all the humans on this earth. He had fought the Soviets at the age of twenty and the Northern Alliance at the age of thirty, without ever ceasing to keep the clans and factions in his territory at bay. Before daybreak, his commandos were going to infiltrate an area that had fallen to the occupation army; their first objective was to punish a disloyal village. He directed all his efforts towards not being noticed by the lookouts who belonged to an advanced coalition operational base, twenty kilometres away from Salavat. Surrounded on three sides, the village was going to suffer the fate of the unbelievers. The perfidy of the local farmers was no longer in doubt, they were nomads who had chosen to settle, attracted by money as well as by the length of the conflict.

They had sold out to the Kandahar drug barons and by the force of circumstances were alienated from the government and a corrupt regional police. The clerics in his group, all champions of small-scale jihad hurtling joyfully towards death, had less sympathy for these miserable farmers than for the wild boar in the hills.

A cock began to crow in the greyness of dawn. Camped in an ambush position on mounds protected by saplings, the column was suddenly distracted by the call of a muezzin. In a jangle of weapons and dishes, they forgot their target to devote themselves to prayer. Slightly apart, Ustad Muhib studied this collection of wattle and daub shacks sheltered by a bend in the low stone walls. They prayed towards Mecca there, as they do here, with no demands of the future. He could make out red sandstone ovens with their pans to bake the bread, work animals and sheep at the back of the courtyards, a dry clay ancestor crouching in the dust, earth soon to be mixed with earth; the crack in a ruin that allowed the branches of a fig tree to enter, pomegranate trees in flower and mango trees with multi coloured rags hanging from them, a mass of amphora placed around an old well surrounded by a rotunda, poultry ambling around in the manure and below, broken down wooden fences beyond which the drying poppy petals quivered like a sea in the distance.

For a moment he blinked at the bluish spasm of the rising sun. It was time. The order to attack unleashed a tempest. While the rebels hurtled down from all over the heights, two missiles and a volley of grenades thrust the village into confusion. On the thresholds of their shacks, the alerted farmers scrutinised the sky before realising the source of the attack. Several fell before their doors; others, armed with antique guns, cursed the enemy shooting blindly. It did not take the insurgents long to break the resistance of a handful of patriarchs. Once they had entered the village, one by one, they shot all the men old enough to fight. The steady rattle of assault rifles threw the houses into panic. Entire families jumped awkwardly out of windows to race towards the roads. The attacker focused his aim on the male silhouettes that fell amidst raised veils and dust. A woman wounded in the neck screamed curses, all the while trying, with both hands, to hold the bright purple scarf in place. More frightened by the screaming than by the blood, two little girls pleaded, sheltering against a wall. Other women fled through the poppy fields and the rocks, following the goats and the sheep. A donkey tied to a post brayed at the centre of the massacre. Grenades exploded in the barns, extinguishing the cries and the tears. Behind a low wall, the Unconscious was the only rebel who had not fired his weapons. Immobile at the heart of the chaos, he held his Kalashnikov with its barrel lowered. The crackle of automatic weapons and the explosions did not seem to affect him. At that moment, he was watching the tragedy as a detached bystander. As if superimposed, other massacres crossed his mind. Nothing forced him to shoot at these people. They were poor poppy milk collectors just like all the others one met everywhere, from the tip of Badakhshan to the Arghandab valley. They reminded him of the farmers in his village in the hollow of the mountains. The donkey continued to bray after the women and children had fallen silent. A cat escaped from an opening. The Unconscious thought he would never see his brother again. Commander Muhib who had just brought down a farmer armed with a pitchfork, noticed him then and went mad. He shouted at him to join the battle immediately, but the child remained inert in the dawn, his gaze fixed on the night of the windows. Arms by his side, he did not hear the orders shouted at him by the rebel chief and his bodyguard with his eagle's profile. Malalaï's beautiful face danced at the edge of a cloud. "Kill him and take away his weapons!" screamed Ustad Muhib. A volley from a Kalashnikov sent the Unconscious sprawling on the bed of ashes and feathers of a barnyard.

The bursts of weapons stopped soon after in a commotion. The commander ordered an immediate retreat. Certainly informed by an observer, the helicopter borne coalition forces were already flying over the mountains. The insurgents fled the dance of the blades at the bottom of the thalwegs. Other aircraft came to land near the buildings. The sun, already high above, drove the last of the clouds beyond the purple gashes of the mountain. The exhausted silence of the mountain, barely broken by a blackbird's call had replaced the racket of the bombs and the rotor blades. Soldiers carried the wounded towards the cabin of a Canadian ambulance craft. The donkey had started braying again. Other shouts, higher pitched, announced the return of the women from the surrounding poppy fields and mountains. Followed by a chaotic horde of children, they rushed towards the corpses laid out along the mosque. Major Helen who had stayed behind with a parachute commando and a male nurse, wandered through the labyrinth to help the last of the wounded hiding in their shacks. While the doctor was seeing to an old man's broken foot, her auxiliary called urgently from a few low walls away. "Helen, quick!" he shouted. She ran across immediately, and bent over the huddled child. "Three bullets at close range", she said. "I thought they only went after men..."

Back from Kandahar, the medical helicopter transported the machine-gunned child, a pregnant woman and the old man with the broken foot towards the civilian hospital. In the emergency ward they did not hold out much hope for the young boy's survival. The bullet that had torn his ear and pierced his neck, explained the coma. But the heart had only been grazed. Two operations left the medical team in a state of hopeful anticipation. On one of the bedposts they had written the name of the village they thought the victim came from and the type of treatment he was receiving. Nobody asked for the boy in the days and weeks that followed. Moved by his fate, Major Helen who had accompanied him to Kandahar after having given him emergency care, came to visit him one morning as she had promised herself. He had just emerged from the coma. Wrapped in his bandages and attached to a drip and a heart monitor, he studied the young woman's fairness from under screwed up eyes, disturbed by the ray of sunlight that made her hair blaze. "What's your name?" asked the major. "You have a name don't you?" He closed one eye and suddenly seemed infinitely sad. Troubled, the doctor wanted to make up for it "It doesn't matter", she murmured. "You'll tell me another day". But as an increase in the number of emergency missions took up all her time, she did not have an opportunity to see him again.

Obviously they did not find his family in the village. The farmers who had survived the massacre had taken refuge in a silence provoked by disdain for the foreigners who were troublemakers in this war, as well as the fear of further retaliation. Once the child had more or less recovered, he was entrusted to a Red Cross home, financed by international aid agencies. The place was overcrowded however, and the shortage of staff made any kind of supervision impossible. A few weeks later he ran away from there, with no risk of being pursued. With neither an identity nor any money, still shaky from the breath of death that had thrust him into an abyss, he went to join the lost crowd in the streets. In other parts of the world, children's eyes are planted in the earth to make a nourishing plant grow. In Kandahar, as in Kabul, children are like weeds that are trampled or pulled up.

Born out of chaos, without even consciously remembering them, he returned to the vagabond habits he had acquired a few years before in a small mining town. To earn the equivalent of half a dollar, he had to accumulate several jobs, crate or empty bottle finder, window cleaner, occasional delivery boy. The competition with the refugee farmers made his task even more arduous. Every day ashy caravans of ghosts arrived, driven out of the sterile countryside.

In the seething bazar area the child finished his day as a beggar after having begun it as a taxi driver's assistant in the ever wary rich areas. He held the arm of a young shepherd, Gulzar, who could no longer see after dusk because of a trachoma brought on by the dryness and glare of the mountains. The man who was intermittently blind had taken a liking to the boy with the torn off ear, and one day he suggested they take a bus to Kabul. There were rich people there who drank Coca cola and smoked *Malboros*. They could save a dollar a day, double or triple, if they got into the opium and cannabis trade or by becoming prostitutes. Enough to leave this hell forever: direction Northern Europe or America. "Why aren't you over the moon?" asked the shepherd who had emerged from his eclipse, one rainy day. "And to start with, what's your name? After all, I'm not going to call you Slave of mercy or Servant of the brave! For the moment you are Zia, my light. I am the rose garden. I would have preferred Massud ..."

In Kabul the competition was a rat race. Street kids, tens of thousands of them, and everywhere the crowds of the impotent and refugees fought over a few Afghanis or a bit of bread. Constantly pushed out of the business area where the Westerners mixed with the local bourgeoisie, Gulzar and his guide tried to slip along the windows filled with the treasures to be found during times of armed peace. There was more to be earned in this perimeter than in the whole town. A tall blond or sometimes, a woman with red hair, her face uncovered, or a chap in fitting canvas trousers and expensive trainers, nonchalantly handed over a dollar, placing it in the hollow of their palm. "Zia, Zia!" the blind man of the evening fervently declared as he woke up another day. "Pity adoption is banned in Islamic countries. You're as bright and handsome as the sunshine, someone would have been delighted adopt you".

At night the two beggars returned to a nearby suburb, a steep area that ran along a river that was a good place to wash. They had built a cabin for themselves out of bits of sheet metal, packing boxes and large dustbin bags. They often found their camp picked apart by people collecting waste paper and scrap metal. Just after daybreak they had to escape the police raids as well as visits from the social services and the Salafist recruiters. And the security agent's dirty tricks or the methodical pillaging by bands of kids intoxicated by glue fumes. Despite everything the dollars piled up. The insignificant population of outcasts and wanderers were familiar with the road transport companies at the gates to Kabul and knew the code name of the escorts who would accept a sizeable payment unknown to the traders. However, only a minority could afford the journey at the back of a trailer truck, in a hideaway carved out amidst the crates of citrus fruit, rolls of carpets or boxes of precious metals. It was better to end up suffocated between two containers than to wait for archangel Azrael, in an atmosphere of general indifference.

A tomb is not a place to die. This is what the Unconscious said to himself shivering in the pitch darkness, a hand on his amputated ear. He listened to the jerks of the road and the panting of thirsty or sick invisible neighbours. Gulzar had been refused at the departure point in Kabul. With dusk he had tripped and the escorts had shouted: "Take your money back, we don't carry handicapped people".

The safest itinerary cannot possibly avoid the opium route, along the border with Sistan-Baluchistan, a southern Iranian province where armed convoys of narco-dealers and contraband fuel dealers file past. To escape being noticed by the militia and other extortionists, to start with, they had to change vehicles at the dead of night in an unknown town. Then they followed the camels in a Baluchi merchant's caravan, along rocky paths at the back of an ancient Berliet filled with tinkling cans of petrol. Another vehicle—an articulated lorry transporting storage containers filled with illegals and a few bundles of opium, jerked its way across desert areas and mountain roads up to the Turkish border. The value of the opium had increased tenfold since the exchange in Afghani land. Once Bulgaria and Albania were behind them, and after innumerable opportunities to lose one's life or end up in prison, they finally reached Italy concealed under the tarpaulins of a dumpster truck. In the hold of a ferry, still imprisoned in a trailer truck, the murmur of the sea replaced the groan of axles. It shifted strangely, like during an earthquake. But this lasted hours. Disjointed images of a ruined past were a distraction from the torture of having no shapes to cling to, stinking and starving in the hollow of darkness. The Unconscious saw emblems flow past—a night of dead stars, ochre fumes of dawn through the flames of a blown up bus, a herd of goats led by a preacher with mad eyes, a pack of dogs or men around a kneeling woman, icy protrusions at the edge of a horizon, night with no memories...

When they reached a deserted square between a luxury hotel and the pyramid of the Ostend station at eleven in the night, the haggard passengers were unceremoniously evicted from the vehicle. An arbitrary decision had been made, the journey stopped there. The cheated illegals had to find their own way to France or England. 'But we paid', shouted one of them. Holding a jack and a crowbar the two escorts had no difficulty making themselves understood. The dumpster truck left after a thunderous u-turn. A guard with a dog was already hurrying towards the young Afghans who had just begun to huddle together after days of solitary confinement. Their bundles under their arms, they raced towards the station. Security guards chased them off before they could reach the waiting area. Behind a fence that ran along a line of warehouses, a beaming kid who seemed familiar signalled to them to follow him. "*Biyaa! biyaa!*" he whispered in the Dari language. He was carrying a string bag himself and he guided the small band towards a partially open cast iron manhole concealed by a worksite. This is how the Unconscious and the other illegals reached the underground galleries and finally, through a last tunnel, the sewers. More than twenty kids, aged between ten and fifteen lived there, lying on cardboard boxes along narrow alleys, beside black water under seeping arches. The only one who could speak a few words of Italian, their saviour was responsible for buying or scrounging victuals up above. Like him, most of the refugees had crossed a part of Asia Minor and Europe, via Iran and Turkey, then Bulgaria or Macedonia, before reaching Italy over the Adriatic Sea. The journey from the Pugila coast to Rome, was a stroll after the misery of a life-threatening expedition. For the first time in months, the Unconscious began to feel a sensation of amnesty or relaxation awaken inside him. Tajiks, Hazaras or Pashtuns, the sewer kids were almost joyful despite the rats and the pestilence. No bomber planes flew over the station. They no longer heard the blast of an attack or the strangled shouts of innocents being pursued. No solemn beard harassed them. With little compassion, the adult emigrants lived apart in the abandoned basements of the station that communicated with the sewers. The Unconscious was amazed that they could live side by side without fighting and abusing each other in such difficult circumstances. His companions laughed often as they nibbled on over-ripe fruit and bread. In the twilight, sustained by means of three oil lamps, cobbled together with a tinder wick and bottle ends, they contemplated these dripping cells where the rats scurried between cess pools and sumps. A Pashtun, three or four years older than him, spoke of France the land of human rights, and Paris, which he had heard of. 'Under the Alam bridge, not far from the Eiffel tower, there are loads of refugees. My brothers are there.' The new arrival had him repeat the name of the bridge and he mumbled it meditatively. He then remembered with fresh amazement, that in another time, he used to be called the Unconscious.

When the railway police and the Italian *Carabinieri* invaded the galleries in force, he had gone off on his own to evacuate his bowels in a run-off tunnel. The only one to escape the net, he left the place a few hours later and wandered around until evening. The air of the streets was saturated with a strong smell of leaves and incense. For fun or out of curiosity, with feline caution he crept into the station area through the main hall and soon found himself on the platforms. A night train was leaving, an express for Amsterdam, via Turin, Lyons and Paris. Paris, this magical name echoed through all the loudspeakers. He did not ponder for long on how had he found himself in a first class compartment, satiated and rocked in the secrecy of a sleeper, facetiously protected by an old Dutch couple. Sleep snatched him away on its wings, taking him a thousand miles from confusion. A Pashtun saying claims that every miracle granted on this earth will be acquitted on Judgement day. But the night carried him far from the warlords, mullahs and the *Carabinieri*, towards the land of human rights.

15

In his role of vagrant, a canvas bag slung over his shoulder, the Roge ventured as far as the canal dragging his feet, far from the brick factory dead end and the rue des Deportés, on the fringes of the perilous Vignes area. Police patrols are not in the least interested in a drunk with his over ripe face. The dealers from below know him by sight, but do not associate him with the Kosovar gang. Like all run down old people, they ignore him out of the corner of their eyes. Back at the dead end, the Roge has garnered enough signals to fuel his predictions. "We're heading for disaster, we should hide the stuff and get out within the hour".

While he encourages information, the Kosovar hates advice. Since his involvement in the artillery sector, a feeling of invulnerability pervades him. Manipulating a Kalashnikov or a rocket launcher reminds him of heroic times. He has always loved weapons. By the age of ten, on the banks of the Ibar in the Leposavic region, he amused himself detonating cartridges stolen from his father, beating them with paving stones or metal bars. Soon after, he transformed a pellet gun so that it shot real bullets. The Kosovo war had arrived to legitimise his games: suddenly he was asked to test his childish dreams... Weapons are as good company as men. But it is only a hobby, a product to lure the customers. Real money comes from gear. Like his competitors in Marseille or in the capital, he nonetheless has an impressive arsenal. Within the space of an hour, with his associates he has emptied the stashes: a false ceiling, a sewer pipe, the nanny's cellar, old graves in the cemetery. Three boxes now contain a mixture of grenade launchers, Scorpio automatic rifles, a muddle of cartridge clips, explosives and inflammatory devices. This equipment is banned however from everyday use. The real amateurs can buy it though, those involved in large scale crime, the clientele from Montreuil or the Champs Elysées, people who hold up vans transporting money, those who extort money from the night clubs and the groups who hold up banks. At their request, the Kosovar finds them a M76 Zastava sniper, an M 80 Zolija rocket launcher, or a M70 assault rifle. Anything they could ever dream of. His suppliers in the Balkans who replenish their stocks from the Serbian or Croatian ex-militia stores or the Armija Bosniac, would be perfectly capable of delivering a tank if he were to order one. However, there is no question of using it in his territory: a few Soviet handheld weapons are enough to scare any kind of aggressor. A jeweller does not go out with his diamonds on him. As for the dealers down below, a mixture of losers and crazies, all they have is probably some modified alarm pistols, some pump action shotguns with sawn off barrels, at best, 12 calibre imitations of Famas or Kalashnikovs, bought for a fortune at the repair shops in Drancy or La Courneuve.

Following his orders, Mehmed has gathered the few loyal people left. He laughs to himself at his boss' pretentions. Apart from Samir and Yann, who are quite annoyed with the canal gang, who is going to support him? The Marches Sèches and the Plateau gave up ages go. All they have left are an old abandoned hick from the colonies, and the angel. Not to forget the junkie, who has gone to the house to get wasted. Nobody left to save face. Just an army with no troops. He has only one thing in mind, to go back to his sis' at Bagnolet, and chase the dragon, alone, in peace with the black fairy. Forget the crack and sister morphine. Nothing like a ball of opium to help change planets.

Back in action, the generator coughs and spits as the lamps blink. In the distance, a factory alarm answers the train whistles. "Okay!" shouts the Kosovar, "as everyone is here..." Emerging from the shadows in the shed, Yann places his foot in a circle of light. "The van is repaired!" he announces triumphantly. And then humbly, "We could take off before they waste us". Crouching next to an extinguished brazier, Alam listens as they speak. The words that had long remained opaque grow clearer little by little. He recognises almost all the words and expressions in this language: balls out, shifty, gun... But he cannot really decipher much of the intention behind them.

A shipwreck like panic reigns in the factory. The canal gang and their supporters have threatened a raid. Nervous, Mehmed even claims it will be bloody. Spitting contradictory orders, the Kosovar seems overwhelmed. He comes and goes, looks out through the bay window at the suburban lights, kneels to check a weapon in the wooden crates, momentarily worries about Poppy. Earlier, when he was suddenly called for, Alam followed him over the shaky footbridge at the back of the dead end. They had hurtled down to the cemetery along a path edged with brambles. They had just heard the closing bell.

In this abandoned area at the very end, just below the brick factory, there are rows of graves with crumbling stucco. One of them, sheltered by an invasive laurel tree, is capped with a bit of metal held in place by the remains of a cement Calvary. Once the smashed slab with 'eternal sorrow' inscribed along the edges is uncovered, the Kosovar signals to the child. The latter instinctively moves away, stopping a fair distance from the hole, remembering how farmers were executed at the bottom of trenches dug with their own hands. A large canvas holdall at his feet, the Kosovar looks at him surprised. "What are you waiting for to get down there?"

It is impossible to disobey a person at whose mercy you are. The smell of an old grave reminds him of spring in the mountains. The earth pierced by roots, crumbles around him. He lifts up a few boards scattered with sand and pebbles. Wrapped in dustbin bags, there are rows of weapons now. Lying on his stomach, his arms outstretched, the Kosovar receives them one by one. The child can make out the dark silhouette of his face at the edge of the grave. He has to cling to the roots to reach his huge hands. Again, the memory of Alam makes him tremble. Which one survived? Which one in the grave ate the earth? Heavier, a missile launcher swaddled in plastic slips out of his fingers and hits his shoulder violently. He catches it by the barrel, biting his lip. Complaining is prohibited; a soldier must never reveal his feelings. He would have liked to tell the Kosovar he will not leave him, that he can be trusted; that he will remain beside him till the end, without a whimper.

In two or three trips in the darkening night, the Caïd and the child shift the weapons to the brick factory. Three pallets of boxes are waiting to be sealed. Mehmed and the two others are walking around them, smoking one cigarette after another. In the opening to a brick oven, the Roge sips from a whisky bottle. The evening silence seems to be interspersed with sounds of rustling. The passerines have fallen silent but some chirp as they dream in the trees. Alam listens to the distant echo of a blackbird. It is the same verse as before. Would there be only one blackbird that has been singing to the world since the beginning of time?

Completely drunk, the former adventurer mutters an ancient air: *During our distant forays Facing fever and fire ...*

His knees pressed together, his head on his fists, Alam surreptitiously observes the Caïd's helplessness. Clearly he is hesitating between putting up a fight and retreat. He notices his abrupt gestures and his sudden moments of dejection. The Kosovar constantly glances towards the doorways, the emergency exits, the low light of dusk through the cement structures. Old Roge stands up tottering, he brandishes his bottle:

Along with our sorrows,
Let us forget death that rarely forgets us
We the Legion.

If he had known how to laugh, Alam would have smiled at least. He is only amazed at the surprising tension in the remaining troops. Mehmed particularly, who sways like a tango dancer, a badly rolled cigarette at the corner of his lips. The West African is watching the rue des Déportés, Samir is on the look-out on the other side. Alam catches the gleam of the barrel of a pump action gun. In the cement frame of a bay window, a slanting flight of swallows and the swaying crown of a poplar stand out against the dark gleam of azure. "What a mean trick!" grumbles Mehmed furious. "We aren't going to wait for them to do us in!" His features drawn, the Kosovar stares at him somewhat exasperated. Without even moving his head, his eyes slide over each of them, as if he has no eyelids, they stop finally at the young boy. "Run and get the decks from the nanny's!" he barks at him. At Alam's stunned expression, he bursts into nervous laughter. "The two packets of powder bring them here to me, the old lady knows what to do. But don't wake up the kid if she's sleeping..."

At the corner of the dead end and the rue des Déportés, a motorcycle shoots past, followed by others. Alam pays no attention to them and goes to Poppy's room. Her kit laid out on the bedside table, she seems wide awake. Almost naked under her tattooed shadow and her piercings, her eyelids half closed, she contemplates the ceiling where rays of shooting stars flow past. Alam bends over and kisses her like a man, at the corner of her lips. The old woman joins him with the packages. "Hurry!" she says. "The cops are patrolling".

There is a commotion at the brick factory. Samir has brought the van closer. They take down the crates of weapons. The Kosovar draws Alam aside, as if to console him. "You're going to have to be very brave", he whispers in his ear. With no transition he orders him to open his anorak, and equipped with a large roll of adhesive tape, he starts to attach the packets of heroin around his chest. Rejoicing at the other end of the factory, Mehmed finishes assembling the parts of a Beretta 92. Alarmed by all this activity, the Roge staggers about not fully understanding. "You, you'll take care of the castle and the lady!" says the Kosovar pushing a handful of crumpled banknotes into one of his pockets.

Yann and Samir on the motorcycle, a Custom Chrome as big as a sedan, Mehmed at the wheel of the van and the Caïd in the dead man's seat, the entire gang from the Vignes area slowly leaves the brick factory dead end. Seated at the back on the boxes of war weapons, Alam mentally runs over his mission: at the slightest incident, run as fast as you can and find a way of hiding the gear in the 'eternal sorrow' grave. A sudden downpour lights the tarmac with the reflection of the streetlights. As they are about to turn, at the corner of rue des Déportés, piercing screams break out behind them in the dead end. It is Poppy, her hair uncombed, a fur jacket open over her camisole; she twists her ankles as she runs on her high heels. "Wait for me! S ... heads, cowards!" she screams, already soaked. Furious, the Kosovar jams his left foot down on the brake pedal. "Just a second!" he says, jumping out of the vehicle without shutting the door.

The crackle of automatic rifles and the champagne cork snap of pump action shotguns make less noise than the trains squealing over the damp rails. Hit in the legs, the Kosovar collapses at the corner of the dead end, without seeing his attackers. Poppy immediately throws herself over him to protect him from the bullets. "It's an ambush!" bellows Mehmed in the second of paralysis that is enough to evaluate one's chances. Taken by surprise, Yann and Samir hurriedly abandon the bike that falls to the ground. Terrified, they respond with sporadic fire, guessing at the direction of their target, while falling back towards the brick factory. A hail of projectiles sweeps the facades. Alone at the wheel of the van, Mehmed seems to realise his luck and he presses down on the accelerator, turning hard left towards the motorway, on the free side of the road. But the machine gun fire gains in intensity. The back tyres are flat and the vehicle has no steering, it skids and hits a tall electrical board that topples over in a shower of sparks. All the street lights in the vicinity go out. With the impact, the heavy cases that have come apart at the back, push the door open. Severely shaken, Alam clings to the metal structure. In the darkness brought on by the electrical failure in the sector, he tries to make sense of the chaos. Dozens of figures appear on the mounds and the low boundary walls. Between two bursts of fire they rush here and there, heads lowered. Gun barrels shine in the rain. He can make out mopeds lying on the ground, several cars blocking the road. Has the war spread to the rest of the world? The Kosovar is bleeding. He cannot get up. In difficulty under enemy fire, Poppy embraces him madly. From the bay windows of the factory, the continuous flash of explosions creates golden halos in the choppy night mist. The West Indian and Samir respond to the heavy fire from the troops lower down. Mehmed has crawled out of the van on his stomach. Under a shower of sparks he grasps his Beretta with both hands. "Stupidity!" he grumbles, not pressing the trigger. Shooting a few random bursts to demonstrate their fire power, the canal gang dealers spread out and draw closer.

With the packets strapped around his chest, Alam has let himself slip to the ground, between the smashed boxes. He has forgotten none of the useful movements. His mission is still just as simple: defend his leader till the end. He knows exactly which weapons to choose: Kalashnikov, rocket launcher, automatic revolver. The cartridge clips join the emerald and the copper casing in his misshapen pockets. Two warheads swell his anorak further. He prays quickly with few words. Alam walks towards the enemy, a sun of death in his eyes. Absent to the world, his mind elsewhere, he is only obeying orders. A low voice murmurs its lamentation deep within him: I do not know how old I am, I am hungry, my heart has stopped. A wolf child he walks with neither fear nor regret. Shooting stars tear through the foliage. When he begins to shoot, a taste of dust and blood fills his throat. He takes the enemy by surprise. Wails of pain erupt, exclamations of fear. A sudden move to retreat towards sheltered positions is accompanied by a series of explosions. Alam does not want to give any ground. With his machine gun he sweeps the mounds and the cars from where volleys of automatic fire emerge. But his cartridge clip is empty. A well-aimed rocket creates a distraction. Two cars explode and catch fire. Alam has recharged his submachine gun. He walks towards the enemy without lowering his guard. Other shouts are audible; bodies collapse. Grotesque shadows run away in the downpour. "It's a madman", shouts someone in the night.

Mingled with the train whistles to start with, the sirens of the police cars grow distinct, increasingly clamorous. Soon a constellation of flashing lights is racing up the avenue de la Deviation and Boulevard Barbusse. Alam advances steadily between the flames and the shadows. The dealer's vehicles burn out. Spurts of sparks that continue to shoot out of the metal board finally set fire to the van. Motorcycles and mopeds start up all over. The order to evacuate seemed to have fallen from the skies. Alam spares those from the canal who try to evacuate their wounded. Nonetheless, new troops, wearing helmets, their guns around their chests, come and gather in places along the rue des Déportés. He is blinded by the dozens of headlights focused on him, Alam must fight. A soldier of God cannot disobey his orders. At the first volley, the police forces retreat chaotically behind the wall of lights. Several officers haul themselves up onto the roof of a van. One of them brandishes a megaphone. "There is no point in resisting, give up your weapons!" but a hail of tear gas follows, contradicting this announcement. The downpour intensifies, cutting through the stagnant gas. Alam ties his scarf around his eyes. In reply he aims a rocket at the wall of vans. The explosion spreads like a firework display. Fire engines and ambulances, other sirens blare in the sector. The blades of a helicopter throb above the train tracks. Before the craft sets down a short way off, the thrust from the rotors disperses the ochre tear gas smoke. Alam thinks of the smooth sleep of the dead. For the first time he sees his brother again, lying on the ground, one hand open, the other placed on his cheek, while a sea of concrete spreads and dust marbles roll in this last shadow. Over there the megaphone issues an ultimatum. A row of shields conceals the assault troops. Alam does not fear them in the least. He was not taught fear. After the rain, an unknown sweetness emanates from the mingled smells of burning and wet grass. His Kalashnikov at the ready, without further ado, Alam begins to empty a new cartridge belt.

The elite sniper commando that descended from the helicopter has quickly taken up position. The precision carabines all focus on the child soldier. Three bullets hit him straight in the chest. He rolls over himself like an antelope brought down in flight. Cries tear through the sudden silence. Her high heels in her hand, Poppy runs barefoot towards Alam, crying, out of breath. "Don't shoot any more!" orders a voice that loses itself in metallic echoes. The young woman has slipped to the ground. Her knees in a pool of blood, she kisses Alam's hair. His eyelashes shut over a wise face, he seems to be asleep. A cloud of dust rises from his chest. 'You killed him!' she weeps, opening his anorak to reveal the torn packets. It is no longer raining. Snow flies in the breeze. Mixed with the blood, in patches it takes on the brown look of resin. "He was a child", Poppy continues to moan. "Just a child". Immobilised by a member of the anti-criminal brigade, she is dragged towards the vans, her face smeared with heroin powder. When Roge, his eyes full of alcohol tears, approaches the corpse, a CRS commando pushes him back unceremoniously. "There's nothing to see", he says. "Go home, go to sleep!" Officers from the judiciary police hurry over. "In God's name! It was a kid!" says one of them, terrified. A petrol tank exploding against the electrical board, illuminates the facade of the brick factory and throws a golden sheet over the tarmac. The fire engine and ambulance sirens blare incessantly. After the routine photographs, one of the civil servants throws a tarpaulin over Alam.